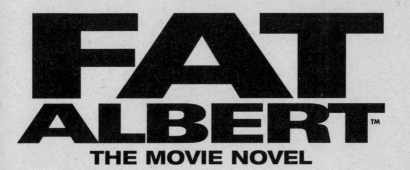

# THE MOVIE NOVEL

TWENTIETH CENTURY FOX PRESENTS A DAVIS ENTERTAINMENT COMPANY / SAH ENTERPRISES PRODUCTION
"FAT ALBERT" KENAN THOMPSON KYLA PRATT AND BILL COSBY COSTUME DESIGNER FRANCINE JAMISON-TANCHUCK
MUSIC BY RICHARD GIBBS MUSIC SUPERVISOR DAVE JORDAN CO-PRODUCER JEFFREY STOTT FILM EDITOR TONY LOMBARDO PRODUCTION DESIGNER NINA RUSCIO DIRECTOR OF PHOTOGRAPHY PAUL ELLIOTT
EXECUTIVE PRODUCERS WILLIAM H. COSBY, JR., Ed.D. CAMILLE O. COSBY, Ed.D. PRODUCED BY JOHN DAVIS WRITTEN BY WILLIAM H. COSBY, JR., Ed.D. & CHARLES KIPPS
DAVIS ENTERTAINMENT    www.fatalbertmovie.com    DIRECTED BY JOEL ZWICK    DOLBY    20 FOX    ©2004  Twentieth Century Fox

Fat Albert: The Movie Novel

Unit photography by Darren Michaels.
HarperCollins®, ▪®, Amistad, and HarperKidsEntertainment are trademarks of
HarperCollins Publishers Inc.
Library of Congress catalog card number: 2004110506
Printed in the United States of America. For information address HarperCollins
Children's Books, a division of HarperCollins Publishers,
1350 Avenue of the Americas, New York, NY 10019.
Book design by Michael Massen
1  2  3  4  5  6  7  8  9  10
❖
First Edition
www.harperchildrens.com

# FAT ALBERT ™

## THE MOVIE NOVEL

By Mike Milligan

Based on the screenplay by

William H. Cosby, Jr., Ed.D.

& Charles Kipps

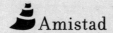
Amistad

HarperKidsEntertainment
*An Imprint of HarperCollinsPublishers*

For Fat Albert, support from family and friends is necessary as young people face obstacles and strive to develop self-confidence. Working hard and helping others is also important in becoming a successful person.

Fat Albert, a delightful fantasy character, continues to be an inspiration and role model for generations of children facing the challenges of growing up. And like Fat Albert, they can have a good time and laugh a lot, too.

Dr. Alvin F. Poussaint, M.D.

PROFESSOR OF PSYCHIATRY, HARVARD MEDICAL SCHOOL
DIRECTOR, JUDGE BAKER CHILDREN'S CENTER IN BOSTON

# PROLOGUE

O nce upon a much simpler time, there lived seven happy, carefree teenage boys. The leader of this group of friends, known as Fat Albert, was a thoughtful young man who always wore a bright red crewneck sweater over a white shirt with dark pants. Whenever there was evil to fight, a wrong to make right, or just some fun to be had, Fat Albert would rally his friends with his favorite cry:

"Hey, hey, hey! It's Fat Albert! And I'm going to sing a song for you. And we're going to show you a thing or two. You'll have some fun now, with me and all the guys. . . . Learning from each other while we do our thing. Hey, hey, hey!"

One of Fat Albert's pals was Old Weird Harold. He wasn't called this because he was older than the others, or because he was really any weirder. Old Weird Harold got his name because he was incredibly tall and incredibly thin, so thin that his shadow was thinner than a strand of spaghetti. Harold didn't have many muscles, but he did have one distinctive talent: He was the only one who could understand every word that Mushmouth said. Mushmouth was another member of the group, and whenever he spoke it sounded like his mouth was stuffed with a peanut butter sandwich or two. For example, if Mushmouth uttered "Hebbie deboe," Old Weird Harold would explain to everyone that Mushmouth had just said "Hello."

Next, there was Bucky, whose two huge front teeth were so sparkling white that folks had to put on sunglasses whenever he smiled. In fact, the only thing that shone brighter than Bucky's teeth was his friend Rudy's ego. Rudy was always perfectly dressed, from the bottom of his stylish shoes to the top of his cockily perched cap. And although Rudy certainly didn't think so, he sometimes looked a little silly in his fancy clothes. But no matter what Rudy wore, he never looked as foolish as Donald, who was never seen without the huge knitted cap that covered most of his face. It was because of this dumb cap that Donald became known as Dumb Donald, even though he really wasn't so dumb at all.

Then there was Bill, who always wore a smile and tried

to make sense of things. But one thing he could never figure out is why his parents, who otherwise seemed to be very nice people, decided to saddle him with a little brother, six-year-old Russell, who always had to go wherever Bill went.

Fat Albert and his friends hung out at their clubhouse in a unique junkyard in North Philadelphia, Pennsylvania. It was a junkyard full of wondrous and interesting things. In the wrecked automobile section, for example, one could see a blue Bronco, a silver Spider, and even a pink Pinto!

As you can probably tell, this was not a normal junkyard. And Fat Albert and his friends were not exactly normal children. You see, they were cartoon characters who lived and played in a colorful cartoon world. They appeared on their own television show every week and were quite content to do that forever. But then, one fateful day not long ago, something happened that changed all that. No one's quite sure what caused it, or if it will ever occur again. But like so many strange things that you read about these days, it's up to you whether or not to believe it.

# CHAPTER ONE
## *Doris and Lauri*

At sixteen, Doris was one year younger than her "sister," Lauri. And although they weren't biological sisters (Lauri was Doris's foster sister), the two teenagers were often mistaken for real sisters. Doris was always surprised when this would happen, because she thought that Lauri was so much cuter and more popular than she was. Doris wished it was as easy for her to make friends as it was for Lauri.

Even so, Lauri idolized Doris. From the moment Lauri moved in with the Robertson family, Doris welcomed her and treated her as if she had been there her whole life. Lauri was so thankful that she had not only gained parents, but also a sister who soon became her best friend. Lauri realized that Doris was a special person, and often wondered why Doris didn't realize it as well. Lately, Lauri had made it her mission to get Doris out of her shell and more involved with life. So far, though, she wasn't sure how well it was working.

One afternoon when the bell signaled the end of fifth

period, the students of Ardsley High School in North Philadelphia poured into the hallways, dawdling, talking, or just plain goofing. But Doris didn't have time for any of that. She hurried out of her classroom and up a staircase as Lauri tried to catch up with her.

"Doris, wait up!" Lauri called as she followed Doris up the stairs, taking two steps at a time. But over the din of the students' chatter, Doris didn't hear her, and by the time Lauri caught up with her, Doris had already started rotating the tumbler of the combination lock on her locker.

"Some of the kids are stopping for ice cream before practice today. Why don't you come with us?" Lauri asked.

Doris knew that Lauri was just trying to be nice. "I'd like to, but I forgot my track shoes. I have to go home and get them. Thanks anyhow."

Before Lauri could try and persuade her to come, Heather and Becky, the two most popular girls in school, passed by on their way to class.

"Hey, Lauri. Are we gonna see you tonight?" asked Heather.

"Yeah, sure," Lauri said.

"Awesome," chirped the two girls in unison.

"We'll see you later then," said Becky as she and Heather scooted off, neither of them even acknowledging Doris.

As Lauri started to open her own locker, she could see the hurt look on Doris's face. "You're going with me to that party tonight."

"Oh, I don't think so, Lauri."

"Come on, Doris . . ."

"Look, I appreciate it, but you don't have to drag me along."

"Drag you along? Doris . . ."

"Really, it's okay. No big deal," she said.

"Doris, what's up with you? Why are you behaving like such a loser?"

Doris didn't answer. As she closed her locker, Lauri struggled to open hers.

"Need some help with that, baby?" said the smooth-talking Reggie Jenkins. Lauri turned to see him standing there with his sidekick, Arthur.

"No, I'm fine," said Lauri firmly. "And don't call me 'baby'."

Reggie laughed at her fire. That's one of the many things he liked about Lauri. And, like most girls he'd gone after, he figured it would be just a matter of time before she came around. "Guess what?" he said, "Heather's having a big party tonight."

"Duh!" said Lauri. "Tell me something I don't already know."

Reggie forced a smile. "Okay, how about this . . . I was thinking you could go with me."

"That's your problem, Reggie," Lauri said. "You get into trouble when you start thinking."

Arthur laughed at this, but quickly stopped when Reggie scowled at him.

Then Lauri pushed past him, hurrying to get to her next class on time. Doris wanted to leave, too, but Reggie blocked her path. He was much taller than she was, and looked down on her with a sarcastic smirk.

"I bet you'd go with me tonight, huh, Doris?"

Even though she knew Reggie was playing her, Doris didn't know how to answer. "I wasn't invited," she said. And then, as she ran off down the hallway, she heard Reggie and Arthur having a big laugh at her expense.

As Doris hurried out of the school, she did everything she could to keep her composure until she got home. She knew that her mother would be at work, and since her father was out of town on business, the house would be perfectly quiet and she'd be able to spend a little time alone before she had to head back to school.

At least, that's what she thought.

# CHAPTER TWO

## *The Plasma Screen*

**W**hen Doris let herself in with her key, she breathed a sigh of relief that she had made it all the way home from school without breaking down. She closed the front door, went into the family room, tossed down her backpack, and flopped onto the couch in front of the new plasma screen television that her father had recently purchased as a surprise for the family. Then the tears that Doris had been holding back began to trickle down her cheeks. She tried to stop them, but that just made it worse and she was soon crying so hard that she didn't notice that she had accidentally sat on the remote control and switched on the television.

And perhaps it was a good thing that Doris wasn't paying any attention to the television. Because if she had noticed, she surely would have found it strange that the television was tuned to a cartoon channel, even though no one in her family had watched cartoons in years. Maybe the explanation was that when Doris sat on the remote, she also changed the channel. Or maybe the family cat had accidentally walked on the remote and pressed the channel button.

Or maybe it was fate.

On the television, Fat Albert's cartoon show was on and he and his friends were involved in a game of buck-buck with their main rivals, a group of tough teenagers. Buck-buck is a game that involves two teams and is played primarily by boys . . . probably because girls are far too smart for such a thing. One team forms a horse, then members of the other team, one by one, run and jump on the horse's back. Whichever team forms the strongest horse that can support the greatest number of the other team's riders without falling, wins. The tough teens had formed their horse and although Bill, Rudy, Old Weird Harold, Mushmouth, and Bucky were perched on their backs, they showed no sign of crumbling. A short distance away, Dumb Donald was preparing to run and jump on their backs. The tough teenagers taunted him, yelling that there was no way he was going to make them fall. With this, Dumb Donald took several long strides, flew through the air, and landed with a thud on the backs of the tough teenagers. The horse formed by their backs sagged. It teetered. It swayed. But amazingly, it stayed up! These were tough teenagers, indeed!

"We beat you, chumps!" they yelled. "We're the buck-buck champions of the world! And that means that from now on, this junkyard is our territory!"

But none of Fat Albert's friends moved. Nor were they worried.

"Bee dotto undo modo bydo," said Mushmouth.

The tough teenagers laughed derisively. "That kid's worse at talking than he is at buck-buck. What'd he say?"

"He said that we have one more guy," explained Old Weird Harold.

The tough teenagers were brimming with confidence. "Bring him on!"

Bucky smiled and called off toward their clubhouse. "C'mon out! We're ready for you!"

The clubhouse door swung open, and the tough teenagers' confidence melted when they saw Fat Albert squeeze through the doorway. "Hey, hey, hey! Buck-buck number seven coming at you!"

And when Fat Albert got down in a sprinter's stance,

ready to run toward them and jump on, the tough teens immediately collapsed.

"We give!" "You win!" they yelled as they scrambled to their feet and ran out of the junkyard. Once again, Fat Albert had saved the day. But that was nothing new for him because everyone knew that whenever there was a problem that needed taking care of, Fat Albert was the person to go to. As they all celebrated their buck-buck victory, an elderly man, Mr. Mudfoot, hurried up to them.

"Fat Albert! I just saw Danielle! She said she was quitting school and running away from home!" Danielle was a character who would occasionally appear on the show.

When Fat Albert heard this, he gathered his friends and told them that they should go help Danielle right away. But before they could leave, they were joined by Russell, Bill's little brother. Like most young ones, Russell loved to tag along with his big brother and his friends. Bill, on the other hand, wasn't so fond of the idea, but always did his best to make sure that Russell was safe and taken care of.

Watching all this on television, Doris was still crying,

but her tears had tapered off a bit as the cartoon characters distracted her. As she stared at the screen, she didn't notice that one of her tears fell onto the remote control. But for some reason, this tear didn't roll off the plastic like the others. Instead, it seeped inside.

Doris continued watching the program as Fat Albert spotted Danielle passing by the junkyard.

"Hey, Danielle, wait!" called Fat Albert.

"Deh, Daboo nello. Wayboo!" added Mushmouth with authority.

Impatiently, Danielle turned to the boys as they approached. "What do you want?"

Fat Albert believed in getting right to the point. "You can't quit school and run away."

"What's it to you?" Danielle wanted to know.

"I care about you."

"Well, don't. Every time someone says they care about me, they wind up leaving me," she said.

"But Danielle, you can't let fear . . ." then Fat Albert suddenly stopped, distracted by something. He listened for a moment, and then turned to Rudy, who was closest to him. "Did you hear that?"

"Hear what?" asked Rudy.

Again, Fat Albert listened very carefully. And soon he heard it again. "That."

And as everyone became very quiet, they began to hear it also . . . the faint sound of crying. But it wasn't the crying of a baby; it was more like that of an adolescent girl. It seemed that somewhere, someone was very, very sad.

"Hey, wait a minute!" barked Danielle. "There's nothing in the script about anybody crying. Now come on, let's get back to what the writers wrote for us. It's your line, Fat Albert, and you're supposed to say . . ."

But as the crying grew louder and louder, Fat Albert and his friends disregarded Danielle and focused their attention on the crying.

Danielle, who considered herself a cartoon character of great importance, wasn't used to being ignored. "Okay, that's it! I'm going to tell my agent to get me on a better show—where people are more professional!" And then, she stormed off the screen.

By now, the crying seemed to be getting closer, but no matter where they looked, they couldn't find the source of the tears.

Then, almost like noticing a shooting star, Fat Albert saw a very small black dot moving toward him. When he pointed it out to the rest of the guys, they hid behind him, frightened, as it got bigger and bigger. But although he had never seen anything like this before, Fat Albert wasn't scared in the least. As the dot got closer, he saw that it wasn't a dot at all, but a big dark rectangle. Although Fat Albert had read about black holes in science, he never thought he'd get the chance to see one up close. Concentrating with all his might, he stared directly into the hole, and before long, he began to make out an image. It was Doris, sitting on her couch, staring at the television and sobbing. That was where the crying was coming from!

As Doris watched from the sofa, she noticed that one of the characters—the big one in the red sweater—seemed to be looking directly at her through her television. She got up and moved nearer to the television to take a closer look.

As she approached the television, her face became bigger and bigger, frightening some of the boys. "It's a monster! It's a monster!" yelled Bucky.

Mushmouth's voice quivered as he said, "Andoo itbee crawlish outibay andob getoo usbee!"

"He's afraid the monster will crawl in here and get us," explained Old Weird Harold, who added, "And I think he's right!"

"I don't think so," said Fat Albert. "She's crying. She needs help."

And then, Fat Albert went right up to the black rectangle and placed his face against it.

In her house, the startled Doris jumped back from the television set.

"Albert, get away from there!" yelled Bill.

"That girl needs me. I've got to help her." Then Fat Albert started to climb into the black rectangle, but Bill and Dumb Donald grabbed him and pulled him back.

"You can't go out there," implored Bill. "This is where we belong. In here. We can't leave this junkyard." Everyone agreed with Bill and pleaded with Fat Albert not to go.

"Look, I appreciate that you're all worried about me. But this is something that I need to do. I can't let that girl go without help. It's just not what I'm about." And then, as the rest of them watched, Albert stepped back from the black rectangle and took a few deep breaths to calm himself. He was scared, but didn't want to show it. Then, quick as the wind, he dashed to the black rectangle and dove in.

But because even the biggest big screen still isn't big enough for a young man of Fat Albert's size to fit through in one plunge, he got stuck halfway.

In her family room, Doris screamed! A cartoon character was sticking out of her television from the waist up! But the part of Fat Albert protruding into her house from the television wasn't a cartoon character anymore. He was a real, live, three-dimensional teenage boy! How could this be happening? Was she dreaming? She pinched herself and winced at the pain. Then she looked at Fat Albert trying to climb out of her TV and screamed again. She grabbed a pillow from the couch and began smacking this curious intruder over the head.

In the junkyard, Albert's friends were desperately trying to pull him back into the safety and security of the only world they had ever known. From Doris's family room, Fat Albert yelled back at the guys to let him go. And then, with one gigantic push, he tumbled out of the television set and into the real world.

As he got to his feet, Doris backed away, frightened. "You stay away from me or I'll call 911!"

"Who's that?" Albert asked innocently.

"Oh, my goodness," said Doris. "This cannot be happening. I'm losing my mind. Yes, that must be it."

Fat Albert walked shakily on his new, human legs, weaving like a newborn baby deer. Then he caught a glimpse of himself in a mirror and was amazed at what he saw. He looked exactly like a normal, although big, human being. He wasn't a cartoon anymore. "Hey, hey, hey! How did I get this way?"

"I have no idea. But you get back in that television right now!" Doris said.

She was pointing at the television when suddenly Rudy flew through the set into the room. He stood and rakishly adjusted his hat, then checked himself out in the mirror. He smiled; he definitely liked what he saw.

"Hello there," he said suavely, introducing himself to Doris. "I'm Rudy. It rhymes with cutie."

After another of Doris's screams, the television screen

was a blur of activity, like a chicken laying eggs, as Old Weird Harold, Mushmouth, Dumb Donald, and Bucky came tumbling out of the set onto the floor of Doris's family room. The whole group was there . . . except for Bill and Russell.

Bill started to climb into the black rectangle that would lead to the human world when Russell whined, "I want to go, too!"

"You're not old enough," Bill said. "Besides, I have a strange feeling that there's something dangerous waiting for us out there." Whenever Bill had a "feeling" about something like that, he was usually right.

"Now go home," he told Russell.

"I'm telling Mom!" said Russell.

As Bill came hurtling into the room, everyone was stretching and bending, trying to get his balance. Everyone, that is, except Doris, who was nowhere in sight. When Bill picked himself off the floor and massaged his back, Doris finally peeked out from her hiding place behind the sofa.

"Is there anyone else?" she asked.

Fat Albert looked around the room. "No, that's all of us."

"Good," said Doris, "now all of you can climb back in there and go back where you came from."

Bill thought that was sound advice. "She's right. We don't belong here. Look at us. This is nuts. We've got to get back."

"You know I can't do that," said Fat Albert. "She has a problem and we have to help her."

"Who said I have a problem?" asked Doris.

"You were crying," Fat Albert reminded her.

Doris didn't feel like talking about why she was really crying, but she certainly wanted to be rid of this odd bunch. Then she got an idea! If she could make up a problem that Fat Albert could solve, they'd probably leave.

"Yes, you're right. I do have a problem," Doris said. "I was crying because, ummm, because . . ." She looked around the room and spotted the backpack that she had just brought home from school. ". . . because I lost my backpack."

Rudy saw the backpack and picked it up. "Is this it?"

Doris, of course, pretended to be very surprised when she saw it. "Yes! That's it! You guys found my backpack!

Thank you very much! Now I don't have a problem anymore!" Then she led them toward the television. "Goodbye! It was nice meeting you. Have a nice trip back!" She tried to hurry them back to wherever they came from, but Albert wasn't convinced.

"Are you sure there's nothing else bothering you?" he asked.

"Positive. I have absolutely no problems. None. Nada. Zero. Bye, now."

Bill turned to Fat Albert. "Problem solved, now let's go home."

They looked toward the television, and the screen showed Russell and Mudfoot still standing there in the junkyard, looking out at them.

"I thought I told you to go home!" yelled Bill to Russell.

"Yeah, but I didn't say I would," said Russell.

"Fine. Then I'm coming back to take you home," said Bill as he moved toward the television.

"And if we hurry, we can be home in time for dinner," said Dumb Donald.

Fat Albert liked the sound of that, and they all followed Bill to the set.

They decided that since Mushmouth was the smallest, they'd help him into the television first. So they picked him up and tossed him into the screen, but Mushmouth simply bounced off it and back into the room.

"Meebee hobbie hoop," whined Mushmouth.

"His head hurts," explained Old Weird Harold.

Doris began to panic. Why wouldn't the television set let them back in? Everyone had an opinion, but then Fat Albert noticed that a commercial had begun.

"That's why," he said, nodding at the television. "We live in the junkyard, not in that commercial. We have to wait until the show starts again." Everyone quickly agreed, amazed at Fat Albert's problem-solving skills.

Doris was particularly relieved that she would be able to bid a final farewell to them in a little more than two minutes. "I'll get you some drinks while you wait."

"I can help," said Fat Albert.

"No! I want you all to stay put, and as soon as your show comes back on, you're outta here." Then she hurried into the kitchen, still a bit woozy from everything that had happened over the past ten minutes. As she removed some sodas from the fridge, she realized that she couldn't tell a soul about this, because no doubt they'd think she was crazy; and she already had a tough enough time making friends. But she did make a mental note to be sure to have a long talk with her father when he returned from his business trip. She'd simply tell him that their new television set needed a guard, or a gate, or some kind of screen so no one could get out of the television. That would make perfect sense, right? Not!

As she turned to go back into the family room, she was so startled that she almost spilled the drinks when she saw Fat Albert and his friends standing in the kitchen, watching her. "Ah! Don't you people make noise when you enter a room?"

The boys considered this for a moment; they had never thought about it before.

"I guess not. Unless the sound effects people make us make noise," said Bill. The others nodded their agreement.

Dumb Donald noticed something on the kitchen counter and became very excited. "Look, another television.

Maybe we can get home that way!"

Doris looked on, astounded, as Donald ran to the small box and began pushing some buttons. The television didn't come on, but the buttons did make strange beeping sounds. "Uh-oh," he said to Doris, "I think your television is broken."

Doris tried to hide her amazement. "That's because it's not a television; it's a microwave."

None of them had ever heard of this before. "Debots ado myoo coe wayboo?" asked Mushmouth. Old Weird Harold could only shrug, because he had never seen a microwave, either.

Doris checked her watch and told them that their show would be starting again soon, so she handed them their sodas and asked them to drink quickly.

But none of them even lifted a can to his lips.

"What's wrong?' asked Doris. "Aren't you going to drink your sodas?"

"Not unless our writers write that we're thirsty," said Bucky. "We once went seven episodes without eating."

"And one time, I did a whole show wearing the same outfit!" said Rudy, who was clearly not happy about that.

"Okay, forget the drinks. The commercials should be just about over and you've got to get back," she said.

They put down their sodas as Doris herded them back into the family room. But when they got there, the closing credits of their show were already running, squeezed into a tiny portion of the screen, with a promo for another animated series occupying the rest of the screen. Doris saw this and began to panic.

"What's going on?" she asked.

"Yeah," added Dumb Donald. "What happened to our show? Why is it so small?"

"I don't know," said Fat Albert, "but I do know that we can't fit in there now."

"Yes, you can! You have to get out of here. Go on, try!" said Doris as she took Fat Albert by the hand and led him to the television. She tried pushing him back through the small area in the screen where his show's credits were still being shown, but there was no way Fat Albert would fit. In fact, there was no way that any of them would fit. She sat on the couch and buried her face in her hands.

Bucky moved to her. "Now do you have a problem?"

Doris looked up at him, not believing that he could ask

such a question. "Gee, do you think?" she asked. "Somehow, I've got a houseful of cartoon characters that I can't get rid of and that I can't tell anyone about. Yes. That might be just a teensy weensy little problem."

Being the most polite of the group, Bill moved to her. "Excuse me, Miss . . ."

"Doris. My name is Doris," she told him.

"Hi. I'm . . ." But Doris didn't let Bill finish.

"I don't care who you are. I just want you gone," she said impatiently.

"No problem," said Fat Albert cheerily. "We'll be gone soon."

"Oh, good," said Doris, relieved. "When?"

"Tomorrow . . . when our show comes on again."

"Tomorrow? What am I supposed to do with you until then?" asked Doris.

"Don't worry. You won't even know we're here," Fat Albert promised.

But somehow, Doris found that hard to believe.

# CHAPTER THREE

## *Seeing Is Believing*

**A**s Doris hurried back to school for her computer class, she still wasn't convinced that everything that she thought happened had, in fact, really happened. When she left her house, her cartoon visitors said they were going out for a walk to survey the neighborhood. Doris couldn't help feeling that, if they really did exist, maybe they'd get lost and be someone else's problem. But for the time being, Doris was relieved to be alone.

As she neared the school, a young boy on a bicycle came her way. "Hey, Doris!"

"Hi, Cody," she said. "How are you?"

"Fine," he said, as he pulled his bike to a stop. Then, a strange smile came over his face. "Who are your new friends?" he asked.

Doris was stunned. How could Cody possibly know anything about them? She soon got her answer when he pointed behind her. She turned around to see Fat Albert and his friends following a short distance back; her knees began to buckle as she realized that they were definitely real, and she wasn't the only one able to see them.

"Oh, uh, they're just friends visiting."

"From where, Venus?" laughed Cody as he rode off.

Doris hurried back to the boys. "What are you doing here? I thought you were going for a walk?"

"We did," said Bucky. "We walked here."

"And for some reason, this neighborhood looks strangely familiar," said Fat Albert, looking around.

Then Bill told Albert and anyone else who would listen, "I don't think we belong outside. We don't belong here."

"We have to be somewhere," said Fat Albert. "We can't get back where we belong until our show comes on tomorrow afternoon."

"Maybe we should go back to Doris's house and wait," suggested Dumb Donald.

"No!" said Doris quickly. She knew that sometimes her mother came home from work early, and the last thing she wanted was her mom walking in to find these weirdos at the house. As Doris fretted about what to do with them, a man passed by, speaking on his cellular phone. Doris thought nothing of it, but this group of misfits was amazed at what they considered his strange behavior.

"Excuse, me, sir," said Bill politely, "but what are you doing?"

The man excused himself from his phone call for a moment, and looked at Bill oddly. "I'm talking into my phone."

"But I don't see any wires," said Bucky.

"Are you yanking my chain?" the man asked.

Bucky innocently circled the man, looking for a chain. "I don't see a chain, either."

"Son, you are weird," the man said to Bucky.

"No, he's Bucky; I'm Weird," said Old Weird Harold.

As the man shook his head and walked away, Doris felt her patience wearing thin. "Don't you guys have anywhere you can go?"

Mushmouth looked at Old Weird Harold. "Doobee loobee noobee woobee."

"Mushmouth wants to know why you don't like us," Harold said to Doris.

Doris looked at the group staring at her sadly. She didn't invite them into her life, so why did she feel so guilty? "All right! All right!" she said to them. "You guys can come to school with me."

"We can?" said Fat Albert, thrilled.

"Sure, why not? Everybody already thinks I'm weird."

"Me, too," Old Weird Harold told her.

"Well, at least you have friends," she told him right back.

Fat Albert heard this and broke into a big smile. "I knew it! You do have a problem. So now all we have to do is find you some friends."

"No!" Doris said, panicked. "Absolutely not!"

"But Fat Albert can help," said Bucky.

"He'll straighten anything out," said Rudy.

Then Bill added, "Albert can talk to anybody."

"Yeah. When Fat Albert talks to people, people listen," said Dumb Donald.

Doris didn't want to hear another word about it. "There will be no talking to anyone about it, understand?"

When the guys finally agreed, they started toward the school. It was her last class of the day and she didn't want to be late. But with this group of oddballs, she certainly didn't want to be early, either.

As they marched along the sidewalk, the guys were amazed at the things they saw in this new world. There were bright and shiny cars that actually had motors! There were tall buildings and big houses. They were so distracted by what they saw that they didn't notice a huge construction hole in their path.

Doris saw it at the last minute and tried to warn them, but she was too late. They fell in, one right after the other. Doris ran to the hole, hoping that they weren't too badly hurt . . . or worse.

But before she could get there, they poked their heads out one by one and continued on their way.

"Nice walking," Doris said to them, laughing. And as they continued toward the high school, everyone was smiling. Even Doris.

Back at the cartoon junkyard, though, things were quite different. Russell was playing on a swing made of an old tire and feeling quite lonely with everyone gone. And Russell didn't get any happier when he saw the group of tough teenagers returning.

"We want a buck-buck rematch because we're gonna

be the buck-buck champions of the world," their leader said in a deep, threatening voice that frightened Russell.

"Sorry, but the guys aren't here right now," Russell stammered. He wondered if he sounded scared, because he certainly was.

"Yeah? Where'd they go?"

"They crawled into this big black square and went into a house in the real world."

The tough teenager glared at Russell, his anger growing. "Do I look stupid to you?" he growled.

Russell wasn't sure how to answer. Then he recalled the rule that his big brother taught him: Honesty is the best policy. "Yes, you do," said Russell.

It was then that Russell learned another valuable lesson: Every rule has an exception. The mean teenager grabbed the tire and pulled it all the way back with Russell still in it. Then he swung it forward as hard as he could, sending Russell flying over the fence.

"Well, boys," he said, "It looks like we just took over this junkyard!"

Doris's computer class was just about to start when she

entered. "Mrs. Forchik?" she said to her teacher. Doris explained that she had some friends visiting and wondered if it would be all right if they audited today's session. It would be only for one day, Doris promised, because tomorrow they'd be gone—long gone.

Mrs. Forchik was a very kind teacher who knew absolutely everything about computers and was happy to pass on her knowledge to anyone who wanted to learn. "Of course they can stay," she said.

Doris looked into the hallway and motioned the boys in. As Fat Albert and his friends looked for available desks, the other students stared at them as if they were from another planet.

Rudy, who was wearing one of his finest outfits, took a seat next to a boy named Darren, who checked out Rudy's spiffy clothes.

"Cool threads, man. Sean John?" asked Darren.

"No, actually my name is Rudy," he explained.

Darren laughed at this, and thought that Rudy was a pretty funny guy. Then Darren held out his hand, palm up, for Rudy to give him five. But Rudy had never seen this move where he came from, so he simply grabbed Darren's hand and shook it.

Nearby, Dumb Donald found a desk next to a student with a high, spiked Mohawk.

"What's that on your head?" asked Donald innocently.

"It's my hair, man," said the student. "What's that on your head?"

"It's my cap," explained Donald, who was surprised that a student in high school would ask such a foolish question.

"Why don't you take it off?" the student wanted to know.

"Because I don't have a face," said Donald.

"Gross!" said the student, who quickly got up and looked for somewhere else to sit. He found a place next to Mushmouth. "How ya doin'?" he asked.

"Hebbie deboe," replied Mushmouth with a friendly smile. Then the student moved again.

Fat Albert was sitting next to Doris when the bell rang for class to begin. Like the rest of his pals, he had picked up the laptop on his desk and was studying it curiously.

"Doris," said Mrs. Forchik, "why don't we begin by having your friends introduce themselves?"

Doris wasn't thrilled by this prospect. "I don't think that would be a good idea, ma'am," she said. "They're very shy."

"I'm not," said Albert, standing. "My name is Fat Albert."

The class giggled at that, but Mrs. Forchik quieted them with a harsh glance. "Nice to meet you, Albert. Doris says you're visiting. Where is it you live?"

"In North Philly," said Albert proudly. The class laughed, and again Mrs. Forchik quieted them with a look. "Was that funny?" Albert asked her.

"Actually, yes," she said, "considering that this high school is in North Philadelphia, which means that you are visiting North Philadelphia from North Philadelphia."

Doris slumped down in her chair, embarrassed. Bringing the guys to school with her was definitely not a good idea. She promised herself that the next time a bunch of cartoon characters jumped through her television screen, she'd know better.

"Do you have anything else to say, Albert?" asked Mrs. Forchik.

"Yes, I do," said Fat Albert. "You see, we're visiting Doris because she has a problem."

Doris sank even lower in her chair.

Fat Albert continued, "She doesn't have any friends so we came here to tell everybody to be her friend."

As the rest of the class chuckled, Doris could feel her face getting hot. She had never fainted before, but she felt like she was getting close.

Mrs. Forchik decided that a change of subject was in order. "That's very nice, Albert. Now let's power-up, log on, and access the Internet."

As the rest of the class started working on their laptops, Doris began to feel better now that the spotlight was off her. Then Dumb Donald raised his hand.

"Yes?" asked Mrs. Forchik.

Dumb Donald held up his laptop. "What is this thing?"

As her classmates hooted, Doris once again felt her face warming with embarrassment. She looked at her watch; there were still twenty-two hours and fifteen minutes remaining before her uninvited visitors would climb back into her television and be gone forever. She hoped she could last that long.

After what seemed like an eternity, computer class finally ended and Doris walked onto the Ardsley High School athletic fields, followed by Fat Albert and the guys.

"Try to behave yourselves," she said, "because you just provided me with one of the most humiliating experiences of my life. I don't have friends because I don't want friends. So I'd appreciate it if you'd please stop trying to help me."

"Wedee arboo sordee eboo," said Mushmouth.

"He said we're sorry," explained Old Weird Harold.

"Yeah," added Fat Albert, "but I can't stop trying to help you."

"Well, try," said Doris as she put on her track shoes. Other track athletes were already on the field, stretching and warming up.

"You run track?" Fat Albert asked.

"The only reason I do it is because my Grandpa ran track for Temple University. It was important to him, so I just run." Then she added glumly, "I'm not very good."

Fat Albert felt like scolding her for selling herself short. "Don't think like that. You can run fast and win. And I'm going to cheer you on!"

"No!" She immediately realized that this might have hurt his feelings. "What I meant was . . . I'd love for you to cheer me on. Tomorrow. From inside the television." But Fat Albert wasn't paying attention, because his eyes were elsewhere.

Across the field, another girl was in her track uniform, stretching. Albert could only stare; he had never seen anyone so beautiful. The artists who drew his cartoon show couldn't possibly ever conceive of someone like her. "Who is she?" Albert asked Doris.

"That's my sister, Lauri. Well, not really my *sister* sister; she's my foster sister. My family took her in last year." Then Doris started off. "I have to go sign in. Just stay put, okay? Don't walk. Don't talk. Don't do anything." And Doris jogged over to sign in with the coach.

Fat Albert didn't watch her go because he couldn't take his eyes off Lauri. Bill noticed this and walked over to him.

"Are you feeling all right?" Bill asked him.

"Never felt better," said Albert dreamily. "I'm going over to talk to Doris's sister." And off he went, his feet barely touching the ground.

As Lauri continued her stretching exercises on the infield grass, an enormous shadow suddenly appeared. She looked up to see Fat Albert standing over her.

He could barely speak. "You're Lauri," he blurted.

"Yes," she said with a smile. "Who are you?"

"I'm Fat Albert," he said.

Lauri was surprised to hear someone say that about himself. "Well, Albert . . . Is there something I can do for you?"

But Albert was so overpowered by her beauty that he could only mumble, "I-ee-oo . . ." Oh my gosh, he thought to himself, I'm beginning to sound like Mushmouth.

"Are you okay?" Lauri asked him.

Albert recovered enough to say "Yeah."

Suddenly a gust of wind blew a piece of dust into Fat Albert's eye and he began blinking rapidly and rubbing it.

"Wait! Don't rub it. You'll only make it worse," Lauri told him.

As Fat Albert lowered his hand, Lauri held his eye open with her thumb and forefinger. He couldn't help noticing that her hands were very soft.

"You have beautiful long eyelashes," she told him. "A lot of girls would be very jealous. How did you get eyelashes like that?"

"Oh, I was drawn that way," he blurted, immediately realizing his mistake. "Did I say drawn? I meant born. I was born that way." He laughed, trying to make light of his slip.

Lauri shrugged, then very carefully looked into his eye and spotted the piece of dust. Then she blew very gently into Fat Albert's eye, getting rid of the speck. "Is that better?"

Albert blinked a few times to be sure. "Perfect," he said.

"My mother taught me how to do that," she explained, remembering a time long ago.

On the other side of the track, two guys in track warm-up

suits were watching Fat Albert talking to Lauri. "No way I'm letting that fat kid get over on Lauri," Reggie said to Arthur. And he intended to do something about it.

Lauri had resumed her stretching exercises, but before long she noticed Fat Albert staring at her again.

Albert was embarrassed at being caught and began babbling wildly. "Doris told me that you two are sisters. I don't mean real sisters, I mean foster sisters. Although foster sisters and real sisters are probably all the same. Of course, I wouldn't know for sure, because I'm nobody's sister. But I guess you knew that."

"Slow down, Albert," she said. "Are you sure you're all right?"

Albert did his best to regain his composure. "Yes, I'm fine but, you see, Doris has a problem, and . . ."

But before he could finish his thought, Doris appeared. "I see you two have met," she said nervously. Then she whispered to Albert, "Did you say anything to her about . . . you know?"

As Albert shook his head no, Reggie and Arthur approached. Reggie slid up next to Lauri and put his arm around her shoulder. "Hey, Lauri. You all warmed up? I like my women warm." He and Arthur laughed.

"Yeah? Well, I like my men polite," Lauri said, removing Reggie's arm from her shoulder.

Reggie wasn't amused at this, particularly when he saw Fat Albert smiling. "Oh, I'm sorry, Lauri," Reggie said sarcastically, "I guess this rather rotund fellow is more your speed."

Lauri scowled at Reggie as the smile disappeared from Fat Albert's face. Albert lowered his head and said, "I'll talk to you another time, Lauri."

As Fat Albert started off, Reggie and Arthur decided to have some fun at his expense. "He sure looks like an athlete, doesn't he, Arthur?" said Reggie.

"Yeah," Arthur laughed. "Do you think he's trying out for the track team?"

"I don't know," said Reggie. "What event could he participate in? Maybe the high hurdles?"

"Or the pole vault," responded Arthur with a teasing tone to his voice.

"I've got it! The long jump!" said Reggie, chuckling.

"Earthquake!" He and Arthur cackled at that.

"Actually," said Fat Albert, turning to face them, "my event is the four-forty."

"The four-forty? They haven't called it that since my grandmother was a baby," said Reggie. "You must mean the four hundred meters."

"Whatever it is," said Fat Albert, assertively. "As long as it has a 'four' in it."

"Yeah?" said Reggie. "How'd you like to race me, beefy boy?"

By now, Fat Albert's friends had gathered around. "You don't want to race Fat Albert," said Rudy.

"Fat Albert? You hear that, Arthur? His name is Fat Albert!" Reggie and Arthur had another big laugh at that.

"He may be fat, but he's fast," shouted Dumb Donald.

Then Mushmouth chimed in with, "Fatbee, butbee fash."

"Is that right?" said Reggie. "Well, what do you say we see how fast you really are?"

Fat Albert smiled. "I already know how fast I am."

"What's the matter, butterball? You have a problem with racing me?" sneered Reggie.

"No, I don't have a problem," Fat Albert said innocently, "I solve problems."

"Well, then, let's see how you solve this one," said Reggie, ripping off his warm-up suit. Reggie's body was solid muscle.

"Albert, you don't have to race him," said Lauri, wanting to save Fat Albert from humiliation.

"That's okay, Lauri, I'll race him," he said. "I just can't take my clothes off."

Reggie was happy to hear that. "Great. Nobody wants to see all that blubber anyway," he said as he and Fat Albert headed for the starting line. "I'll race you once around the track, if you can make it that far," Reggie said as he got down in the starting position. Fat Albert tried to do the same, but his stomach prevented it. "It looks like somebody could use a head start," smirked Reggie.

"Okay," said Fat Albert. "If you feel you need one."

"I meant *you*," Reggie said. Then he turned to Lauri. "So, if I take it easy on your pudgy pal, will you go to Heather's party with me tonight?"

"Let me think about that," said Lauri. Then, without thinking, she said, "Nope."

Reggie was getting aggravated. "Fine. Then he gets no mercy."

As Reggie and Fat Albert prepared to start, Rudy said, "On your mark, get set, go!"

And Reggie took off like he was shot from a cannon, leaving Fat Albert at the starting line. Albert looked to his friends. "Gee, he is fast," he said. Then he started off after Reggie, jogging at an easy pace.

Knowing that he left Albert in the dust, Reggie ran smoothly and confidently, head up and smiling. So imagine his surprise when he heard a voice right behind him.

"You're doing very well, Reggie. You're a very good runner."

Reggie turned and was amazed to see Fat Albert right on his heels, running effortlessly. "Oh, yeah? Well, wait till you see this," Reggie said. And then he began to run even faster. He turned around and, as he expected, Fat Albert was no longer right behind him.

"Running is great exercise," said Fat Albert, who was now running right next to Reggie! Fat Albert was running backwards; and he wasn't even breathing hard!

Then Fat Albert turned around and sped away, leaving

a straining Reggie in the dust. By the time Reggie crossed the finish line, Fat Albert and his friends were with Lauri and Doris, waiting for Reggie to finish. Fat Albert got up and walked over to Reggie, who had his hands on his knees, gasping for breath. "You know, Reggie, just because you came in second, doesn't mean that you're not a winner, too." Then Fat Albert tried to shake Reggie's hand.

But Reggie would have none of it. "You haven't seen the last of me, fat man," he sneered.

"Yeah," said Arthur, "Reggie's nobody to be messing with." Then he helped his defeated friend to where the coach was gathering the team.

Lauri smiled at Fat Albert. "I'm glad you beat him. He deserved it. But how did you do it? You were amazing."

"Yeah," said Bill. "I've seen you run fast before, but never like that. What happened?"

Fat Albert looked at Lauri, and thought he knew the answer. But he wasn't ready to share it just yet. "I don't know. It must have been something in the air."

Fat Albert would have liked to spend the rest of the afternoon with Lauri, but Mr. Gillespie, the track coach, called for her and Doris to join the rest of the team.

As they ran off, Fat Albert watched Lauri go, a huge smile on his face. Deep, deep down inside, he felt something that he had never felt before. And, although he couldn't be sure, it seemed like it was some kind of human emotion. He didn't know what it was, or where it came from. But he did know one thing: He sure liked it.

# CHAPTER FOUR

## *No Problems*

**A**s the guys walked down a street in Doris and Lauri's neighborhood, Fat Albert was still on cloud nine.

"Do you think Lauri likes me?" he asked no one in particular. "Even though I'm fat? I mean, it's the person who matters, not how they look, right?"

"Beats me," said Rudy.

"Yeah," said Bucky. "None of us ever had a girlfriend before."

"Eyebee nebee tahdee to a girbee uldee," said Mushmouth.

Old Weird Harold explained that Mushmouth said that he had never even talked to a girl before.

"And why do you want just one girlfriend anyhow?" asked Rudy, puffing out his chest and straightening his hat just so. "You're never gonna see me having just one girlfriend."

"Never say never," said Fat Albert with a grin. "The thing is, I can't explain the feeling I had when she blew in my eye," he said, staring at the clouds. "It was like a gentle summer breeze, blowing over a cool lake and . . ."

"Okay, that's enough," Bill said. "Albert, you have to focus. We're here because you have to solve Doris's problem. No other reason. And we have until tomorrow at two thirty, so we better put our heads together."

"Like this?" asked Dumb Donald, touching his head to Bill's.

"What I'm saying is, once we solve Doris's problem, we need to get back to our world right away. Or am I the only one who's noticed that we . . ." Bill stopped himself, not wanting to alarm the others until he was absolutely sure that his fear was correct.

"That we what?" asked Fat Albert.

"Uh, nothing," said Bill. "Forget it. Let's just solve Doris's problem and get back to where we're supposed to be, okay?"

As they thought about this, they noticed a group of high school students heading their way. Leading the group were Heather and Becky, both wearing their cheerleader outfits.

"Loobee," said Mushmouth, "twibees."

"No, they're not twins," said Old Weird Harold. "They're cheerleaders."

Fat Albert had an idea. "Cheerleaders are the most popular girls in school," he said. "All we have to do is get them to be friends with Doris and that will solve everything."

Heather was telling her group a story, monopolizing the conversation as they passed by.

"Excuse me," Fat Albert said to Heather.

"Yeah?" she said, not happy at being interrupted. "Who are you and what do you want?"

"I'm Fat Albert," he answered.

"You sure are," said Heather. The students laughed. "What can I do for you?"

"Well, it would be great if you could be friends with Doris," he said to her and Becky.

Heather and Becky looked at each other and tried to keep from laughing. "Us, be friends with Doris?" asked Becky. "You're kidding, right?"

"No," Fat Albert said. "You see, Doris doesn't have any friends, so we have to fix that."

"Awwwww, isn't that sweet?" Heather said sarcastically.

"Tell you what: Why don't you guys come to my party tonight?" she asked. "Daddy's blocking off the whole street. Bring Doris. She should have so much fun." As the other girls laughed, Heather and Becky moved off down the sidewalk.

Fat Albert smiled to his friends. "See? I told you! Hey, hey, hey, Fat Albert always saves the day." And as they started off, laughing and joking, Bill lagged behind and observed them closely. He hoped that his fears were wrong.

"You did what?" Doris screamed.

"We talked to Heather about your problem," Fat Albert told her.

She got up from the computer and closed the utility room door. Her mother was still at work, but if she came home Doris didn't want her to hear strange voices. "I can't believe you did that!" Doris said.

"You don't have to thank us," said Dumb Donald. "Fat Albert will always save the day."

"I don't want to hear any more 'saving the day' stuff from any of you!" Doris said. "Exactly what part of 'I don't have a problem' don't you understand?"

"Of course you don't have a problem now," Fat Albert said with a smile, "because Heather invited you to her party tonight."

"And she invited us, too," crowed Rudy. "Isn't that cool?"

"Well, have a good time," said Doris. "I'm not going."

"Buddee shebee realbee wandbee youdee todo combee," said Mushmouth.

"That's right," said Old Weird Harold, "she really did want you to come."

"Why? She didn't want me to come before." Doris returned to her homework on the computer. "Besides, I don't have anything to wear."

Fat Albert realized that reasoning with Doris wasn't going to work. Then, he got an idea . . . perhaps a little negotiating would do the trick. "Well, if you don't go to that party tonight, we won't be able to solve your problem," he said. Then he winked at his pals, "And if we don't solve your problem, I don't see how we can go home tomorrow."

"Are you threatening me?" Doris asked.

"Only if it works," Fat Albert said with a smile.

Doris knew she had a tough decision to make. If she went to the party, she knew it wouldn't go well. It never did. But if she refused to go, these guys might stay around forever.

"Well, what do you say?" asked Fat Albert. "Are you going to the party?"

"No," she said, as their faces dropped. "Not until I go to the mall and get something decent to wear."

When they heard this, they cheered. And Fat Albert cheered the loudest, because he knew Lauri would be at the party, too.

# CHAPTER FIVE

## *It's a Mall, Mall World*

**A**s they started to enter the mall from the street, Fat Albert and his friends hesitated.

"What's wrong?" asked Doris.

"I've never seen such a big window," said Dumb Donald.

"It's not a window," explained Doris. "It's a glass building." And then, after she assured and then reassured them that it was safe, they all went inside.

When they entered the mall, there were so many new and wondrous things to see that they didn't know where to look first. As they headed for the escalator, they passed through the Food Court.

"What are all those wonderful smells?" asked Bucky.

"It's food," said Doris. "They have pizza, hoagies, Chinese, ribs . . . Whatever you want." She saw that they were thoroughly enjoying the aromas. "You must be hungry. When was the last time you ate?"

None of them responded right away, as they seemed to be thinking. Finally, Bill spoke up. "I think we all ate about two years ago, when we did that show where everyone came to my house for dinner." The rest of them immediately remembered that and complimented Bill on his mom's cooking.

Doris couldn't help laughing at this. "The store I need is upstairs," she said. As they headed for the escalator, Fat Albert noticed a clothing store that just might have something especially for him.

"You go ahead, everybody. I'll catch up with you in a minute," he said.

Doris went up the escalator while the rest of the guys went their own separate ways.

Fat Albert hurried toward a clothing store for big and tall men.

Once inside, Fat Albert was amazed at the variety of clothes. There were silk slacks, corduroy coats, and even velvet vests! As he perused the racks and racks of garments, a salesman approached.

"Have I got something for you!" said the salesman, who certainly seemed to have a lot of energy. "Something free," he added.

Fat Albert liked the sound of that. "What is it?" he asked.

From behind his back, the salesman produced a brand new Philadelphia 76ers cap. Fat Albert thought that he would look good in that cap, and felt that Lauri might think so, too.

"Why, thank you," Fat Albert said, reaching for the cap.

But the salesman pulled it away. "If you're looking to buy, then I am your guy. All you have to do is talk to me, and you get the cap for free." The salesman beamed, because he had written that himself and was extremely proud that he was able to make it rhyme. Then the salesman removed a sport coat with large black and white checks from a hanger. "Now this," he said, "is you!"

Fat Albert looked at the coat, and imagined that if he wore that to the party, he'd look like a chessboard with legs. "Do you have anything in blue?" he asked.

"Excellent," said the salesman, "that's just what I was thinking!" And he showed Albert a dark blue jacket with gold buttons. "Let's try it on," he said as he took it off the hanger. "You'll need to take off your sweater."

Fat Albert backed away. "No, no, I can't take off my sweater."

"Why?" asked the salesman.

"Because I don't know what's under it." When he saw the salesman looking at him curiously, Fat Albert tried to explain. "You see," he said, "I'm not really a . . . Oh, never mind."

The salesman was not to be deterred, so he helped Fat Albert put the jacket on over his red sweater, then led him to a mirror. Fat Albert liked what he saw and wondered what Lauri would think.

Then Fat Albert tried on more jackets, and ties, and scarves, and sunglasses. When he was finally done, his arms held a pile of clothes that was so big that it hid his face. The salesman finished adding up all the price tags.

"That will be three thousand, four hundred, twenty-eight dollars and twenty-two cents. "Would you like to pay cash?" he asked.

"Oh, no," answered Fat Albert, stunned.

"Fine. Then what credit card will you be using?" the salesman wanted to know. "I don't have a credit card," Fat Albert said.

'That's all right, sir. We can open a store account for you. All we'll need is your Social Security number," said the salesman.

"I don't think I have one of those, either," said Fat Albert.

"You mean you can't buy any of this?" asked the salesman, who looked like he was about to cry.

"I guess not," Fat Albert responded apologetically.

Then the salesman took all the clothes from Fat Albert, including the 76ers cap.

"Wait a minute," said Fat Albert. "You didn't say I had to buy; you just said I had to listen."

And with that, Albert took back his free cap. "Thank you and have a nice day," Fat Albert said. And he exited the store, whistling merrily.

As Fat Albert walked through the mall, he was overwhelmed by the wonderful colors and sounds of the place. This certainly was an exciting new world! As he passed a music store, he saw Bucky and Rudy inside, both wearing earphones. So he went inside to see what they were doing.

Once inside the store, Albert was amazed at all the records in there. But the only thing they had in common with the records he had back in the junkyard clubhouse was the hole in the middle. These new records were very small and were a shiny silver color, not black like his. And from what he could tell, they weren't made out of vinyl, either. Fat Albert strolled over to Bucky and Rudy. "Hey, guys," he said. But they couldn't hear him because of the earphones, so he tapped Rudy on the shoulder. Rudy removed his earphones. "What are you listening to?" asked Albert.

"It's called a CD," said Rudy. "I think this one is music, but they're not really singing; they're talking." Then he showed Fat Albert the album cover. "It's something called 'hip hop.'"

Fat Albert put on the earphones and gradually began getting into it, moving to the rhythm. And then he started grunting and adding some lyrics of his own. When people began staring, Rudy removed the headset.

"What did you do that for?" asked Fat Albert. "I was really feeling it."

"I heard," said Rudy. "And so did everyone else in here."

Fat Albert looked around and saw everyone staring at him. A bit embarrassed, he gave the earphones back to Rudy and left the store with a big "Hey, hey, hey!"

As Fat Albert continued his tour of the mall, he spotted Old Weird Harold, Mushmouth, Bill, and Dumb Donald at a kiosk that sold the very latest in cell phones and cell phone gadgetry. The saleswoman was demonstrating a phone that could also take pictures.

"Okay, my friends, this is the best mobile phone–digital camera combination on the market today," she said. "Not only can you phone, page, text message, and access the Internet, you can also shoot crisp, download-able digital photos in full color!" She aimed the device at Old Weird Harold and Mushmouth. "Smile and say 'cheese,'" she instructed.

"Cheese," said Old Weird Harold.

"Chebodeebos," said Mushmouth.

And the saleswoman snapped their picture. Then she attached the phone-camera to a digital printer and announced, "Your picture will be ready in five seconds. As you can see, the XFP 2500 is the ultimate communications device of 2004!"

"2004?" said Dumb Donald. "What happened to the Seventies?"

"They became the Eighties." she told him. "Where

have you been living? Under a rock?"

"Of course not," said Donald defensively. "In a junk-yard!"

The saleswoman dismissed this as foolishness as she retrieved the photo from the printer and handed it to them. When everyone saw the photo, they "ooohed" and "aahhed" at the sharp color. Everyone except Bill, that is; because when he looked at the photo, the familiar look of worry came over his face again.

"I knew it," he said.

"Knew what?" asked Fat Albert.

Bill knew what he was about to say should only be heard by the guys, so he led them away from the kiosk over to a quiet corner of the mall. "Look at the photo," he told them. "What do you see?"

"Old Weird Harold and Mushmouth," said Rudy, studying the picture.

"But do you notice anything strange?" asked Bill.

"Like I said . . . Old Weird Harold and Mushmouth," Rudy repeated, laughing. They all slapped hands at that.

"We don't have time for jokes," said Bill. "Look at the color on the picture. See how vivid it is?"

"Yeah, it's perfect," said Bucky, and everyone agreed.

"Exactly. The color is perfect; it's exactly how Mushmouth and Old Weird Harold should look," said Bill. "Now look at them standing here. They're losing color."

"Whash?" said Mushmouth, alarmed, as everyone crowded around to compare the picture to the real thing. And one by one, they agreed that they did seem to be fading just a bit.

"Hey, hey, hey!" said Fat Albert, trying to reassure them. "It's just a picture. Pictures aren't real."

"Neither are we," Dumb Donald said.

"I can't believe I'm saying this, but Dumb Donald is right," said Bill. "We aren't real. And I think that living in the real world is making us fade."

Fat Albert suspected that Bill was right, but to calm the others he said, "No, man, we're not fading. It's just the light." Then he held his arm up in an uncomfortable, contorted position. "See? If I hold my arm like this, it's not fading."

Then everyone but Bill held their arms and legs in weird positions to convince themselves that Fat Albert was right.

"Yeah," said Rudy, "it's just the light."

"We're fading, I tell you," said Bill. "We need to get back to our world as soon as possible."

"But it's fun out here," said Rudy.

"What about our world? We always had fun there, too," Bill reminded them.

"Look," said Fat Albert, "I'm sure it's no big thing. We're going back tomorrow anyhow. So let's stop worrying about it and have a good time at the party tonight!" he said happily. "What do you say? Hey, hey, hey!" And for now, everyone but Bill was satisfied.

As they moved away from the kiosk, Doris approached, carrying a large shopping bag. "You ready to go?" she asked them.

"Did you buy something to wear?" asked Donald.

"Of course I did," Doris said. "What kind of teenage girl would I be if I went to a mall and didn't buy anything?"

"Can we see it?" asked Rudy.

"Yes, you certainly can," Doris said. They all gathered around, waiting for her to take her purchase from the shopping bag. "But not until later," she said with a smile.

"Now let's go. If we have to go to that party, we might as well be on time."

Bill looked at his friends as they happily left the mall. Then he looked at the picture of Old Weird Harold and Mushmouth. No doubt about it, he thought. They were definitely fading. He just hoped that by the time their show came on tomorrow, it wouldn't be too late.

# CHAPTER SIX

## *Party On!*

That evening, in the park across the street from Doris's house, Fat Albert and the guys waited for her to come out in her new dress. They had been waiting inside, but Doris heard her mother's car pull into the driveway and snuck them out the back door just in time!

Doris didn't like hiding things from her mother, but this was an extreme situation that would never happen again . . . she hoped.

Finally, the front door opened and Doris came out. She looked beautiful; the dress she bought looked perfect on her. As she crossed the street, though, she couldn't help feeling self-conscious and more than just a little unsure of herself.

"Well?" she said nervously. "How do I look?"

"Spectacular," said Rudy, looking into her eyes. And then something happened. Doris looked into his eyes as well. And Rudy's eyes told her that he wasn't just being nice; he really meant it. And for that brief moment,

Doris felt really good about herself. As for Rudy, he was totally smitten with her.

"Well, let's get going," Fat Albert said, breaking into Rudy and Doris's thoughts. And then he started off down the sidewalk, walking a lot faster than everyone else. After all, Lauri was already at the party.

The street in front of Heather's house had been blocked off to traffic, and the party was in full swing when they arrived. Albert looked over the crowd and spotted Lauri, sipping a soda. He went over to her; "Hey, hey, hey!" he said.

"Oh, hi, Fat Albert," Lauri said with a sincere smile. "I'm glad you came."

"Really?" asked Fat Albert.

"Really," said Lauri. "You're very nice." Then she softly patted his cheek.

Fat Albert staggered at the touch of her hand on his face, and his legs felt like they were turning into wet noodles.

"I'll go get you a soda," he said.

Lauri laughed. "I already have one," she said, indicating her orange drink.

"Then I'll go get myself one," said Albert, who moved off with some pep in his step and glide in his stride.

As he walked toward the refreshments, he passed by Arthur and Reggie, who eyed him suspiciously. "I knew it!" said Reggie. "Lauri came to the party so she could be with that fat kid."

"I think you're right," Arthur said dutifully.

"Shut up!" Reggie told him. "I don't want to be right." Then Reggie whispered something to Arthur, and Arthur smiled devilishly. Reggie's plan would surely make Lauri see Fat Albert for what he was—a big, fat loser!

When Fat Albert got to the refreshment stand, he noticed someone hiding behind it. And she was wearing a brand-new party dress. Albert went back to investigate. "What are you doing back here?" he asked Doris.

"Go away!" she said in a loud whisper.

"No," said Fat Albert, refusing to budge.

"I don't think coming here was such a good idea. I should go home," she said.

"No way," Fat Albert insisted as he grabbed a soda. Then, very gently, he said "C'mon, Doris, go for it."

Something in Fat Albert's voice caught Doris's attention. She wasn't sure what it was; but it stirred memories of someone from a time long ago.

"Now let's go," he said, leading her out from behind the stand. "You've got some partying to do."

"Some party," Doris said glumly. "Nobody ever dances with me anyway."

At this, Fat Albert offered his arm. "They will tonight," he said. And as much as he wanted to get back to Lauri, Fat Albert knew that dancing with Doris was the right thing to do.

On the dance floor, Fat Albert danced with complete confidence, performing moves that drew the attention of the other dancers. Doris started tentatively at first, unsure of herself. But as Fat Albert urged her on, she gained confidence and began dancing in a way that she always knew she could, but until now had been afraid to try. For the first time in a long time, Doris began having fun.

Just as she and Fat Albert were getting into a groove, Reggie grabbed the microphone and the music stopped. "Hey, y'all!" yelled Reggie, and the crowd shouted back to him. "I've got a big, fat treat for you tonight!" he continued. "And coincidentally, his name is Fat Albert!" As the crowd murmured, Arthur smiled wickedly, knowing what was to come.

"Come up and say a few words to everyone, Fat Albert!" There was a challenge in Reggie's voice.

Doris didn't want Fat Albert to be humiliated. "Don't do it, Albert," she pleaded, knowing that Reggie only wanted to embarrass him.

"Why not?" said Albert. "I'm proud of who I am."

As she watched Fat Albert climb onto the stage, Doris wished that she had that kind of confidence.

Reggie handed the microphone to Albert. "What do you have to say, big man?

Albert studied the microphone, then said to Reggie, "I say: Where's the cord?"

The crowd laughed at him for this. Doris cringed, and wished she had been able to stop Albert from going up there.

"It doesn't have a cord, my oversized friend. This is 2004 on earth, but I'm not sure what year it is wherever you live!" he said with a laugh. The crowd enjoyed this and laughed along with him.

"Neither am I," Fat Albert said into the microphone,

seeing what Reggie was trying to do. "Now, how'd you like me to sing you a song?"

"Yeah, we'd like that a lot, wouldn't we?" Reggie called to the crowd. Reggie was certain that any song that Fat Albert sang would make him the laughingstock of the party. Then Lauri would see how foolish she was for hanging around with this bucket of blubber.

Albert began singing to the tune of his show's theme song. "Hey, hey, hey! It's Fat Albert!" Then he nodded to the DJ, who changed the beat from old school to the freshest hip hop, just like the music Albert had heard at the mall.

"Ey-oh, I'm gonna sing a song for you," Fat Albert sang. "And, oh, we're gonna show you a thing or two. We'll have some fun now with me and all the guys. . . . Learning from each other as we do our thing. Say ey-oh!"

And, to Doris's surprise, the crowd responded with an enthusiastic "Ey-oh!"

On the stage, Reggie couldn't believe what was happening as Albert continued. "They call me Albert, that's my name, and solving problems is my game! Now get it jumping if you're feeling what I'm saying, no delaying!"

And now, even the DJ was caught up in Fat Albert's rap. "Ey-oh, big Al, he makes you feel all right. So shake your body at the party tonight!"

Fat Albert held the microphone for another five minutes, revving the crowd with his hip hop lyrics, and when he finished, they gave him a wild standing ovation! Then Fat Albert hopped off the stage, slapping hands with everyone in sight.

"Well, thank you, my man, for rocking this town," said the DJ as he put on a slow record. "Now DJ Jake is gonna slow it down!"

And when the DJ put on a slow song, Fat Albert extended his arm to Lauri and led her onto the dance floor where they began to dance, nice and easy . . . and close.

Reggie was furious that his plan had backfired; and when he saw Lauri dancing with Fat Albert, he knew that she was just trying to make him jealous. Well, he thought to himself, two can play that game!

To the side of the dance floor, Rudy was talking with Doris. But Rudy wasn't his usual cocky self. There was something very sincere about him when he was with Doris. He had never felt this way about anyone before. As he was about to ask her to dance, Reggie appeared.

"Hey, sweet thing, want to dance?" asked Reggie.

"No, thanks," said Rudy, misunderstanding. "I'm talking to Doris."

"Not you," he said to Rudy as he nodded to Doris. "You."

Before Doris could respond, Reggie took her hand and led her onto the floor. Doris felt happy that a boy had finally asked her to dance, but she was also very nervous about it. Dancing with Fat Albert was easy, but she didn't know what to expect from someone like Reggie. Doris didn't notice Rudy's sad expression as he watched her with Reggie, who had maneuvered the two of them very near to where Fat Albert was dancing with Lauri.

As they danced, Reggie kept moving closer to Lauri, hoping to get her attention. But she never so much as glanced at Reggie. This upset him even more, so he decided to do something that would guarantee that Lauri would pay attention to him: He pulled Doris close and tried to kiss her.

Doris was taken by complete surprise, and she tried to be gentle when she pushed Reggie away. "No," she whispered.

But Reggie wasn't about to take "no" for an answer. He had to make Lauri jealous, so he tightened his grip on Doris and tried to kiss her again.

"Reggie, please don't," she said, a little louder this time.

"Come on, baby. Don't be like that," Reggie said as he gave it another try.

Then Doris yelled, "I said stop it, Reggie!" She shoved him away. This got the attention of the people around them, who stopped and stared. Doris felt her face getting warm again; she knew that coming to this party was a bad idea. She turned and ran off the dance floor.

Reggie yelled at her as she disappeared into the crowd. "You should be happy I danced with you at all!"

Rudy had been watching the whole thing from the sidelines. It was time to defend Doris. He walked up to Reggie, ready for a confrontation.

Reggie looked down at him, "You got a problem, shrimp?"

"Yeah, I do. And you're it!" said Rudy. Rudy prayed that Reggie would back down, because he knew that he didn't stand a chance against someone with all those muscles.

Reggie stared at Rudy and was about to grab him when he suddenly stopped. Rudy wasn't sure what had happened until he heard Fat Albert's voice right behind him.

"Rudy, be a gentleman," Fat Albert said. "Go see how Doris is doing."

After shooting Reggie a final snarl, Rudy left to find Doris.

Then, Fat Albert became more serious than he had ever been before. "You stay away from her," he advised Reggie, "or you'll be dealing with me."

Reggie and Fat Albert stared at each other, not moving a muscle, as the crowd waited to see who was going to back down. And before long, Reggie blinked and backed off. "This isn't over," he warned Albert as he walked away.

Fat Albert turned to see Lauri standing nearby and moved to her. "That was very nice, Albert," she said. "Now I better go find Doris."

"Don't worry," he said, taking her hand, "Rudy's with her."

And as the rest of the guys watched him and Lauri talk, they all agreed that Fat Albert looked out of the ordinary. And it wasn't just the fading, which had become a little more obvious. It was something totally different.

Finally, Mushmouth offered an explanation. "Heeby duby lum," he said.

Old Weird Harold didn't like what he heard. "You take that back!" he said to Mushmouth.

"What did he say?" asked Bill.

"He said that Fat Albert is in love."

And none of them could argue with that.

Later, Doris was at her front door, ready to go in, as Rudy stood at the bottom of the steps, trying to reason with her.

"But we thought we were helping," he said.

"Helping what?" she asked. "I don't have a problem. I was doing just fine before you guys arrived." And then she stormed inside, slamming the door behind her. Rudy had never felt so sad; he wished there was something he could say to tell Doris how he really felt. He was crazy about her.

On a nearby street, Lauri was walking home with Fat Albert. "I've decided I don't have time for relationships," she said. "People say they care about you, and then they

Doris has been having trouble making friends at school.

Fat Albert climbed out of Doris's TV set and straight into her living room!

Doris takes her new friends to class.

What are these things?

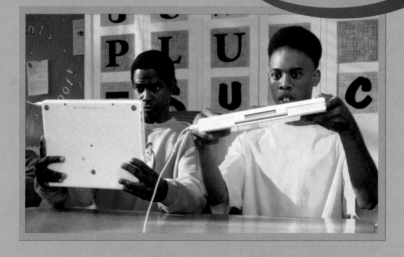

Reggie challenges
Fat Albert to a race.

Hey, hey, hey!
Fat Albert's winning!

Fat Albert and Doris arrive at the big party.

Fat Albert gets down on the dance floor.

Will Mr. Cosby be able to help Fat Albert?

The guys need to go back home before they fade away!

Fat Albert can't leave Lauri and Doris just yet . . .

. . . not before he solves Doris's problem.

Doris finally realizes she's a winner!

Fat Albert says good-bye to Doris.

wind up leaving you. You can't trust them."

Fat Albert knew that deep down inside, she didn't really believe that. And even if she did, she could certainly trust him. He decided to tell her so, but before he could say a word, Lauri continued.

"Anyway, I'm better off working on my writing," she said. Albert was surprised to hear that she had dreams of being a writer. "Ever since I was a little girl," she said, "I've wanted to tell stories. Personal stuff," she told him, suddenly aware that she had never felt comfortable enough to share this with anyone before. "You know, maybe about how a person feels because their parents . . . are no longer around." Her voice began to quiver.

"I'm sorry," said Albert. "I know it must be hard."

"I miss them a lot," she said. "Sometimes it hurts so bad that I don't want to care about anyone again." Realizing that her eyes were tearing up, Lauri wiped them with her sleeve.

"Don't worry, Lauri. I'm here." He looked up and noticed they had reached her house.

"Thanks for walking me home," she said as they walked up the steps.

"My pleasure," said Fat Albert. Lauri took out her key, but Albert took it from her. "Allow me," he said, then unlocked the door for her.

"Thank you. You are such a gentleman," she said as he handed her the key. She started inside, then stopped and turned back to him. "Albert," she asked, "you and I? BFF?"

"BFF? What's that?"

"BFF . . . Best Friends Forever," she explained.

And with that, she gave Albert a kiss on the cheek and went inside. When she closed the door, Albert put his hand to where she had kissed him. Then he took his new 76ers cap from his pocket and put it on, slightly off center, as he bounded down the steps. And as he headed into the warm summer night, he didn't know where he was going. And he didn't care.

Fat Albert walked around the city all by himself for a while, basking in the wonderful feeling that the evening had given him. This was certainly a different world—full of different emotions—than the one he was used to.

Then he thought about Bill's concern about them fading, and looked at his arm. He had to admit that his bright red sweater might just be a little bit paler than normal, but he was sure that it was nothing to worry about. Then Fat Albert looked up ahead and saw his friends standing on a bridge, looking down.

As he approached, Rudy pointed to something below, amazed. "Look! It looks just like our junkyard!" he said. Dumb Donald had led them to this spot. There, below Philadelphia's old Ninth Street Bridge, was a junkyard that looked exactly like their cartoon junkyard, although it was not nearly as colorful. But Bill was the only one who noticed that.

# CHAPTER SEVEN
## Day Two

The next morning, the guys were in the park across the street from Doris's house, waiting for her and Lauri to leave for school. And although none of the group talked about it, they realized that they had become paler overnight. After a while, Doris came out of the house and started toward school. The boys crossed the street and joined her.

"Good morning, Doris," said Rudy politely, straightening his clothes to look his best for her.

"Hi, Rudy," she said, looking him over. "Are you all right?"

"Yeah, fine. Why?" he asked.

"You look so pale. Like you're faded or something," she said. Then she looked at the rest of them. "You all look the same way. Are you sure nothing's wrong?"

Bill started to speak up, but Fat Albert wanted to change the subject. "No, we're all terrific," Fat Albert said. "We were waiting to go to school with you and Lauri." Then he tried his best to be casual when he asked,

"By the way, where is Lauri?"

"She's tutoring a ninth grader, so she went to school early today," Doris told him. As Fat Albert tried to hide his disappointment, Doris stopped walking. "I don't think it's a good idea to come to school with me today. People are starting to get suspicious."

"Hey, that's okay. We understand. Right, guys?" said Fat Albert, and they agreed that they'd find something else to do.

"Why don't you hang out in the park?" she suggested. "That way, you'll be right here when I come home at two thirty to send you off." And then she headed off toward school.

Rudy watched her go, and called, "Have a nice day, Doris."

Doris looked back, smiled, and waved. Then the guys crossed the street to the park, which had a basketball court and a play area for children. Fat Albert, Bucky, Dumb Donald, and Bill headed for the children's area, where there were four metal horses mounted on springs. As they played cowboys and sang western songs, Rudy, Old Weird Harold, and Mushmouth moved to the basketball court where a game of two-on-two was in progress. Another player was standing by himself, watching the game from the sideline.

"Hey, Old Weird Harold," said Rudy, "you're pretty tall. How come I've never seen you play basketball?"

"Because the writers never let me," Old Weird Harold said with a touch of regret. "I've got a feeling that I might be pretty good, though." And the last word was barely out of his mouth when an errant pass came whizzing toward him.

"Duhkuhbee," yelled Mushmouth, warning him.

But to the surprise of everyone, Old Weird Harold deftly caught the ball with one hand. "No problem, Mushmouth," he said. "I didn't need to duck."

That brought the watching basketball player over to them. "Hey, man, you want to play?" he asked Old Weird Harold. "We need another player for three-on-three."

"Sure, why not," said Harold. Then he got up to join them.

"Bedee carboofulsh," said Mushmouth.

"Don't worry about me," said Old Weird Harold with newfound confidence. "Something tells me they're the ones who should be careful." And he walked onto the court and joined the other players.

Over at the play area, Bill and the others had finished their horseplay. "What do you want to do now?" asked Bucky.

Fat Albert looked over to the basketball court and saw Old Weird Harold preparing to play. "Hey, hey, hey! I've got a basketball game to watch! C'mon." And Bucky and Bill followed. But Dumb Donald had other plans.

"You guys go ahead," he said. "I'm going to the school library."

"Library?" said Bucky. "You can't read."

"I can now, I think," Dumb Donald said as he started off.

"Okay, but don't be late. Be back by two thirty," Bill reminded him.

Dumb Donald nodded and went on his way as the rest of them sprinted over to the basketball court to join Rudy and Mushmouth. And as they watched the game, they couldn't believe what was going on: Old Weird Harold was a superstar! On offense, he dribbled behind his back, between his legs, then dunked the ball over two defenders! On defense, he made steals and blocked shots just like a professional player! The guys were amazed and soon began chanting, "Old Weird Harold, he's our man. If he can't do it, no one can!"

Nearby, a mother was watching her little girl play with a balloon when a slight breeze blew the balloon over to Mushmouth. As the others continued their cheering, Mushmouth picked up the balloon and took it back to the little girl.

"Hebbie deboe," he said as he handed the balloon to her.

The little girl frowned at him. "What did you say?" she asked.

"Hebbie deboe," Mushmouth repeated.

The little girl looked at him curiously for a moment, then figured it out. "'Hello?' Is that what you said?"

"Yebbee," responded Mushmouth.

"You talk funny," she said. Then she held up the balloon. "Do you know what this is?" she asked him.

"Baba looboon," he answered proudly.

"No," she said patiently. "Baa-loon."

"Baa-loo-boon," he said.

"No, silly. Ba-loon," she said slowly. "Balloon."

"Balloon," Mushmouth said.

"Yes! That's it! You got it!" she yelled, excited.

Mushmouth was thrilled. "Balloon, balloon, balloon! Thank you. Thank you. This is great!" And for the first time ever, he didn't need Old Weird Harold to interpret what he was saying. In his excitement, he ran over to the little girl's mother. "Ma'am, it has been my extreme pleasure to meet your little girl. She is exceptionally bright."

"Why, thank you," said the little girl's mother.

"Good-bye," Mushmouth said to the little girl.

"Goodup byebee," she answered with a wink and a smile.

Then Mushmouth hurried over to rejoin his friends to watch the rest of the game, which ended when Old Weird Harold blocked his opponent's shot, picked up the ball, dribbled all the way down the court, and scored the winning basket with a thunderous slam dunk!

Old Weird Harold shook hands with the other players and ran over and joined his friends.

"Amazing!" said Fat Albert.

"Incredible!" chimed in Rudy.

"That was the finest exhibition of basketball skills this young man has ever witnessed," said Mushmouth.

Then there was a stunned silence as the guys turned to Mushmouth in disbelief.

"That was you, Mushmouth?" asked an astonished Bill.

"That's right, William," said Mushmouth proudly. "And from now on, please don't call me 'Mushmouth' anymore."

"What should we call you?" asked Bucky.

Mushmouth gave it some thought, then told them that "Mouth" would be just fine.

"And I don't want to be 'Old Weird Harold' anymore, either," said the new basketball star. "I'm 'Air Hal' now," he said, twirling the basketball on his finger. Bill couldn't believe what was happening to them. But then again, maybe he could.


As Doris entered the school library to look for a book she needed to complete an essay, she noticed Dumb Donald sitting at a table, a stack of books in front of him. She hurried over to him.

"What are you doing here?" she whispered.

"Reading. I'm on volume twenty-two of African American history. There's some very interesting stuff in here," he told her.

"I know," she said. "But I thought you were dumb."

"That was when I was a cartoon, I guess," he said. "But now I'm feeling pretty smart. But I bet I could read a lot faster without this cap."

"Then take it off," Doris said. And before Donald could stop her, she removed his cap. "Why do you wear this thing? You have a very nice face," she told him.

Dumb Donald was stunned. "I do? I have a face?" And then he felt his face. It was a real face, with cheeks and a forehead. "I do have a face!" he yelled excitedly. "I have a face! A nice face!" And he yelled so loud that the librarian had to shush him.

"Keep reading while I check out a book," Doris told him. "Then we'll leave so we can be home by two thirty," she said. And as she walked over to a bookshelf, Dumb Donald spotted a computer that wasn't being used. He carefully stared into the monitor and then he saw it . . . a reflection of his face! Dumb Donald was overjoyed! This new world truly was a miraculous place. But Dumb

Donald's happiness ebbed as he continued looking at his reflection in the monitor. Because there, right before his own eyes, he saw himself fading ever so slightly.

And then, Dumb Donald ran from the library.

Back at the park, the guys were hanging out, waiting for 2:30 to arrive, when Bill noticed something very strange and startling. "Oh, no!" he cried out.

"What?" asked Fat Albert.

"My hand!" cried Bill. "Look at it," he said as he held it up to the sun.

They all looked up at his hand and saw something truly amazing . . . and frightening. If they looked very closely, they could see the sun showing through Bill's hand. "See? I told you," he said. "We're fading away."

"We're not just fading," said Mushmouth. "We're becoming translucent." As they looked to him for an explanation, he continued. "That means that we're losing so much color that light is beginning to shine right through us."

The rest of the guys checked themselves and, sure enough, it was beginning to happen to them, too.

"I'm scared," cried Bucky, who was playing on the

merry-go-round. "I want to go home!" But he jumped off while it was still spinning, and skidded along a strip of pavement on his rear end. And while he was sliding, the others noticed that behind him, he was leaving a long green skid mark that was the same exact color as his pants. When they helped him up, they saw that the skidding had worn through the seat of his pants. And because there was nothing drawn underneath, Bucky now had a huge hole in him that the others could look through!

"I can see the basketball court!" yelled Old Weird Harold as he looked through the hole where Bucky's rear end used to be.

"You look like some magician sawed you in half!" added Rudy.

"It's like I'm in two pieces," Bucky screamed, covering up the hole by pulling down his sweatshirt. Everyone could see Bucky was worried, but nobody knew quite what to do about it until something occurred to Fat Albert.

"Let's go," he said. "I have an idea."

And they all hurried from the park, with the guys crowding around Bucky so he wouldn't scare anyone.

When they arrived at the junkyard under the Ninth Street Bridge, Fat Albert immediately spotted something he had seen there earlier—a discarded can of green paint. He called Bucky over and started to paint the seat back onto Bucky's pants. But it wasn't working—the paint had nothing to stick to! This made Bucky panic even more, and he told Fat Albert that all he wanted was to get back to his cartoon world where he could have his pants back and be a whole person. Then Fat Albert checked his watch: 2:35! They were already late! And they tore out of there as fast as their rapidly fading legs would take them.

At Doris's house, the television was tuned to their program as Doris paced nervously, checking her watch. "Where could they be?" she asked Dumb Donald, who still had his cap off and was on the sofa, reading one of her Advanced Placement science books.

"They'll be here. I know they will," he said, not even looking up from the book.

On the television show, Russell had returned to the cartoon junkyard, sneaking around and trying to stay out of sight, when he was spotted by the leader of the other boys.

"There he is!" yelled the leader. "Let's get him!" And the boys chased after Russell, who turned and began to run away. But they were gaining on him fast, and he needed a place to hide. Up ahead he spotted an old beat-up convertible with a closed canvas top. He ran to the car, opened the door, jumped in, and locked all the doors, leaving one window slightly open for fresh air.

When the mean kids got to the car they tried to open the doors, but couldn't. "Come out of there, you little runt!" their leader yelled. The teenagers tried everything to get little Russell out of the car, but nothing worked.

"That's okay by me," said the leader. "He's got to come out sometime. And when he does, we're gonna play buck-buck!" Then he looked through the windshield into Russell's frightened eyes. "That's right . . . All my guys against you! And then this junkyard will be ours! All ours!" Inside, Russell felt tears welling up.

As Doris continued to pace in front of the television set, Fat Albert, Bill, Bucky, Old Weird Harold, and Mushmouth came rushing in. "It's about time!" Doris said. "The show's almost over!"

But Doris's television set wasn't the only one tuned to

the show that afternoon. On the sidewalk outside a television store in North Philadelphia, two guys were watching the show through the storefront window.

"Interesting viewing," Reggie said to Arthur. "Are you thinking what I'm thinking?"

"I'm always thinking what you're thinking," said the loyal Arthur. Then he asked, "What are you thinking?"

"I'm thinking that there's something strange going on," Reggie told him.

Then it started to rain in the cartoon junkyard, and the mean teenagers ran off, looking for shelter from the storm. After making sure they were out of sight, Russell rolled down a window and screamed, "Help!" Then he jumped out of the car and ran up to the screen, talking through the television. "Fat Albert, you have to come back from the real world fast! Please! Jump back into that Doris girl's television set and get back here before they take over our junkyard. And our show!" Then he ran and jumped back into the convertible and rolled up the window.

"Don't worry, Russell," Fat Albert said from Doris' family room. "We're on our way." Then Fat Albert turned to the guys. "Bucky, you first. You're the one with your you-know-what hanging out."

The group circled Bucky and led him toward the television. Then he dove through. When he landed safely in the cartoon junkyard, Fat Albert and the others cheered and whistled!

And Bucky was happy, too, because the seat of his pants had immediately returned. And there was more good news, too! "Look!" Bucky said happily through the screen. "I'm not faded anymore! All my color is back!" And the guys in Doris's house saw that it was true.

"Okay, who's next?" asked Fat Albert.

"I'll go," said Old Weird Harold. "With my new co-ordination, those fools don't have a chance at beating us at anything!" he said confidently. Then he dove through the screen into the junkyard and landed with a thud. He picked himself up awkwardly, then took a step and tripped over a tin can. He picked up the can, spotted a nearby trash can and tried to make a basket. When the can missed by a mile, he realized that his athletic ability had deserted him. "Oh, well," he said, shrugging, as he looked into the screen. "It was fun while it lasted."

Dumb Donald volunteered to be the next to go. "I'll go. I'm smart enough now to understand that we're fading away because we're in a world where we don't belong. And when you try to become something you're not, you lose the essence of who you are." Then Dumb Donald stood there for a moment, pondering his brilliance.

"Go," said Doris.

"Right," answered Dumb Donald, who then dove through the television screen.

Dumb Donald tumbled into the junkyard; but when he got up, Bucky, Old Weird Harold, and Russell began screaming!

"Eyeballs!" shrieked Bucky.

"Floating eyeballs!" added Old Weird Harold.

Dumb Donald soon realized why they were so frightened. Without his cap on in the cartoon world, he had no face! His eyeballs were just floating! So he took his cap from his back pocket and pulled it over his head. And presto! He was back to his old self.

"All right, Bill, your turn," Fat Albert said.

"I want you to go first," Bill responded.

"Me? Why?" Fat Albert seemed a bit uncomfortable.

"Because," said Bill, "I want to make sure you really go."

There was an uncomfortable moment as Fat Albert chose his words carefully. "Bill," he finally said, "I've decided that I'm going to stay."

"No, you're not," said Bill, pushing Fat Albert toward the television.

"Yes, I am," said Fat Albert, pulling away.

And then, Doris suddenly screamed, "Nooooooo!"

"What's wrong?" Bill asked her.

But Doris could only point at the television screen. Just like the day before, the credits were running on the side of the screen. She knew that Fat Albert, Bill, Rudy, and Mushmouth had missed their opportunity.

The guys saw that Doris was disappointed. "Hey, hey, hey," Fat Albert crowed happily, trying to cheer her up. "We can make it through another day!"

"And how do you know that?" asked Bill. "You've never faded before."

"We'll be fine," said Fat Albert, even though he didn't really believe it.

"You don't care if we're fine," said Bill. "You just care

about staying with Lauri." From Fat Albert's reaction, Bill knew that he had hit a bull's-eye.

"It's not just that," said Albert. "I haven't solved Doris's problem yet, either."

"I do not have a problem," insisted Doris, waving her arms.

"Do, too," said Fat Albert.

"Do not," insisted Doris.

"Too!" said Albert quickly

"Not!" replied Doris.

They kept at it until the door opened and Lauri entered. "Hi. What's going on?" she asked.

"Uh, nothing," mumbled Fat Albert. Doris kept quiet.

"Where are the rest of the guys?" Lauri asked.

"They went back," said Bill without thinking.

"Back where?" Lauri asked.

Mushmouth started to blurt out, "Into the . . ."

But Doris interrupted him just in time and noticed that Lauri had something in her hand. "Are those tickets to something?" Doris asked her.

"Yeah," said Lauri. "They're free passes to the fair tonight. I already checked with Mom and she said we could go as long as we're not out too late. Any of you want to come?" Then she smiled hopefully. "Albert?"

"That would be fantastic!" he said, smiling back at her.

"How about you, Doris? Want to go?" asked Rudy hopefully. Doris didn't seem at all enthused about the offer.

"I don't know. I want to make sure I get enough sleep before the big track meet tomorrow."

"Please? I promise you'll have a good time," he told her.

Like before, Doris looked into Rudy's eyes and saw that special look. All of a sudden, she couldn't resist. "You know, I would. I'd love to go, Rudy."

"Yes!" said Rudy, unable to contain his excitement.

# CHAPTER EIGHT

## *My Fair Ladies*

At the Ninth Street Bridge junkyard, Fat Albert, Bill, Rudy, and Mushmouth noticed that their fading had gotten worse and that they were becoming more and more translucent. They finally admitted that there was a good chance they might not last through the night, not to mention until tomorrow so they could go home.

"All I want is one final night with Lauri, that's all. And I want it to be the best night ever," Fat Albert said. Then he left for Lauri's.

"Poor guy," said Bill. "I wish we could do something to make his last night one he'll always remember."

"One that all of us will remember," added Rudy.

"Fat Albert should go to the fair in style," Mushmouth said. Then he spotted several nearby junked cars. "And I do believe that I've had an inspiration that just might do the trick."

Later at Doris and Lauri's, the girls came out of the house with Fat Albert. They both looked beautiful, and Albert thought that they would probably be the most attractive girls at the fair. As they started down the front steps, they heard a familiar voice calling.

"Ladies, your chariot awaits." It was Rudy, standing at the curb beside a patchwork quilt of a car they had thrown together at the junkyard. One door was black, another was orange, the hood was blue, and the rest of the car was the color of rust.

"What is this?" asked Lauri as they approached.

"A car," said Rudy. "It's one of a kind."

"Let's hope so," Lauri said with a laugh.

Fat Albert and Rudy held the doors open for the girls, with Lauri getting in the front seat, and Doris in back. Then Rudy climbed in next to Doris, and Fat Albert sat behind the wheel.

"Okay, Albert, let's roll," Rudy said.

Fat Albert couldn't believe that this old crate would actually run. "You mean, start it up? Are you sure?"

"Trust ol' Rudy," he said. "Go on. Turn the key."

Albert did and immediately they all heard a sound coming from under the hood. Although it sounded a little like a car motor, it sounded more like someone imitating the sound of a car motor.

Doris and Lauri exchanged puzzled glances.

"Okay," Rudy told Fat Albert, "give her some gas."

Fat Albert stepped on the gas pedal and to his utter astonishment, the car began moving forward.

"Buckle up, girls," said Rudy. "We should be there in no time."

As the girls fastened their seatbelts, they still had the feeling that there was something just a little bit different about this car. And they were right, because under the car, on recliner bicycles, Bill and Mushmouth pedaled as fast as they could, taking turns making their best engine noises.

At the fair, Fat Albert and Lauri shared a chair high atop the Ferris wheel. From their vantage point, they could see almost all of Philadelphia. "It's beautiful up here, isn't it?" said Fat Albert.

"It sure is," she said. "I'm having a really good time tonight, Albert." Then Lauri patted the stuffed brown teddy bear that sat on her lap. "And thanks for winning this for me."

Fat Albert beamed. "Hey, hey, hey! Any time of day!"

And he and Lauri giggled like a couple of little kids.

In the chair just below them, Rudy sat with Doris. "These have been the two greatest days of my life," he told her. "I know it's been kind of a bother for you, but . . ."

"Hey," Doris said, stopping him. "You can bother me any time."

After the Ferris wheel, Fat Albert and Lauri decided to go on the roller coaster. It looked scary, but how scary could it be?

Fat Albert got his answer soon enough when the rickety coaster plunged down the first hill. He was so frightened that when he opened his mouth to scream, nothing came out. Lauri, on the other hand, was laughing the whole way, and when the ride ended, she poked fun at him for being so scared.

"I wasn't scared," Albert fibbed. "I just looked scared because my cheeks wrapped around my ears and my eyelids went up over my head."

Lauri laughed and kissed him on the forehead. Albert thought he was going to melt.

While Lauri and Albert were on the roller coaster, Rudy and Doris sat at a small, quiet table away from the action of the fair. As they laughed at the strip of black and white photos they had just taken, Rudy turned to Doris.

"Let me ask you a question," he said. "If I didn't have to go back . . . if I were a real person . . ."

"But you're not," said Doris.

"I know. It's just that you make me forget who I am. I was just wondering," he said nervously. "If I were a real person . . . Would you?"

Doris knew exactly what he was asking. But he was so cute when he was nervous, she couldn't resist keeping it going for awhile longer. "Would I what?"

Rudy took a deep breath, summoning all his courage. "Would you go out with me?"

"You mean on a date?" Doris asked.

Rudy nodded.

"The way I see it," she said, "we're already on a date."

That had never occurred to Rudy. "Yeah, we are, aren't we?" he said with a big smile. "All right!"

"And if you were a real person," Doris went on, "this would be the first of many."

Rudy knew he didn't have a real heart; but if he had, it certainly would have skipped a beat. He extended his hand across the table and Doris put her hand in his.

This was a very good night.

Fat Albert was waiting for Lauri to get off a ride that spun round and round. The roller coaster was one thing, but the Big Spin was quite another. As he sat on a bench, he noticed that a ten-year-old boy was staring at him. "Hi," said Fat Albert.

The boy approached, "You're Fat Albert!" he said excitedly.

"Hey, hey, hey!" said Fat Albert.

"What are you doing here?" the boy wanted to know. "You need to get back to your TV show. These bad guys keep chasing Russell, and you should be there to help him. He needs you; we all need you," the little boy pleaded. "If you're not there, who's gonna solve all the problems?"

Fat Albert stared at the boy, deep in thought, as the boy's father arrived.

"Come on, son, we have to go," his father said, taking the boy's hand.

"But, Dad, I was talking to Fat Albert," said the boy.

The father was immediately embarrassed. "Mind your manners," he told his son. Then he turned to Fat Albert.

"I'm sorry. I, uh, I think that because he's so little, to him everyone looks fat. I mean overweight. I mean . . . Come on, son, your mother's waiting for us."

As the boy left with his father, he turned back to Fat Albert. "Hey, hey, hey," said the little boy happily.

"Hey, hey, hey," Albert responded, trying to sound happy himself. But he wasn't happy, because he knew what the little boy said was true.

Then Fat Albert noticed Lauri and Doris standing in line at the Sno-Kone booth and went over to them. As he approached, he couldn't help overhearing their conversation.

"Do you think something's wrong with them? Lauri asked Doris. "They seem . . . I don't know . . . paler than they did yesterday."

"Maybe they just put too much bleach in their clothes," Doris answered.

"I hope nothing's wrong with Albert," Lauri said. "I mean, I think this is real. He's charming, bright, and such a gentleman."

Fat Albert beamed and tried to get a little closer. He didn't want to miss a word of this.

"And he's the first guy I've met in a long time I feel I can trust . . . the kind who will always be there for me." When Albert heard this, his face dropped. But Lauri had more to say, "He's not the kind of guy who will be nice to me tonight and be gone tomorrow."

Those words took his breath away, and he realized that he had created a huge problem for himself, and an even bigger one for Lauri. And for once in his life, the big problem-solver had no idea how to fix it.

# CHAPTER NINE

## *Fat Albert Meets His Maker*

After the fair, when the guys were back at the Ninth Street Bridge junkyard, Bill, Rudy and Mushmouth were sitting on the porch of the clubhouse. But Fat Albert was sitting on the roof, all alone and staring off into the distance.

Bill examined his own hand; by now it was so faint that it was very hard to see. "I just hope we're not completely faded before two thirty tomorrow. We've got to make it back into that television set."

"I can't go back. I didn't solve Doris's problem," Fat Albert said as he climbed down the ladder. "And worse, I caused a problem for Lauri; so I've got to stay until I can work that out."

Bill had heard enough. "You can't stay, man! You're fading just as bad as I am! You want to turn into a big pile of powdered celluloid? We live on film, Fat Albert, and once we fade away, we're gone forever. Is that what you want?"

But Fat Albert didn't answer. He just walked away into the night.

"Fat Albert, where're you going?" called Rudy.

But Fat Albert wasn't sure where he was going, or why. It was as if he was being led somewhere . . . somewhere he'd been a very long time ago, back when he was first created.

He walked for hours, but it was only when he found himself in this neighborhood of large homes that Fat Albert felt that somehow, he was nearing his destination. And when he spotted the beautiful mansion, something led him up the long driveway toward the front door. He stepped onto the porch and, after taking a deep breath, he rang the doorbell. Albert didn't know who lived here, but when he heard a man's voice coming from inside, it was a voice he knew that he had heard before.

"I'll get it, sweetheart," said the man's voice. Then the voice got closer to the door, "Who is it?"

"It's Fat Albert and . . ."

"Very funny," said the man on the other side of the door. "Listen, it's not Halloween, so you can't be trick-ortreating. So whoever you are, you better be gone by the time I count to three. One . . ."

"No, really, my name is Fat Albert. I'm sorry to bother you, but . . ."

"Two . . ." said the man from inside.

"It's just that I feel I have to be here, and . . ."

"Three!" And then the man opened the door.

When Fat Albert saw who the man was, his jaw dropped. So that's why he was led to this particular house. Of course; now it all made sense. This was the only man who would have all the answers.

"Mr. Cosby!" Fat Albert stammered.

"That's right, son," said Bill Cosby, the famous comedian and educator who created Fat Albert and his friends. "And who are you?" Mr. Cosby asked.

"It's me—Fat Albert! Really!"

"Oh, is that right?" Bill Cosby said, humoring his visitor. He was used to this, because a lot of people did Fat Albert imitations when they met Bill Cosby.

"Well, if you're Fat Albert," Mr. Cosby said, "then let me hear it."

But Fat Albert was stumped. "Hear what, sir?" he asked.

And in his best Fat Albert voice, Bill Cosby said, "Hey, hey, hey!"

Fat Albert smiled, then said, "Hey, hey, hey!" right back. And he could tell that Mr. Cosby was beginning to believe him.

And Mr. Cosby thought that the young man standing on his front porch sounded exactly like Fat Albert. And he had obviously done his homework, because he was dressed exactly like Fat Albert, too . . . except for one very important aspect.

"If you're Fat Albert," Bill Cosby asked with a smile, "how come you're so faded?"

"That's why I came here, Mr. Cosby," Fat Albert said, "You see, what happened was . . . Aw, it's a long story."

Bill Cosby stared down at this young man and noticed that his face was full of sincerity. Then he did something that surprised even himself. Bill Cosby sat down on the top step of his front porch and made himself comfortable. "That's okay, friend," said Mr. Cosby. "I like long stories."

So Fat Albert sat next to him and told him his tale, and Bill Cosby listened to every word. And as Fat Albert went on, Mr. Cosby couldn't help thinking—even as unbelievable as his story might be—that maybe Fat Albert was telling the truth.

"So you see," concluded Fat Albert, "I don't want to be Fat Albert in some cartoon anymore. I want to be Big Al in the real world."

Mr. Cosby could see that Fat Albert was very upset over his predicament, and knew that he had to be very gentle with him.

"Albert, I think you know that you've got to go back," he said. "I just wish I could figure out what brought you through the television in the first place."

"I heard Doris crying," Albert said.

"Doris? Who's Doris?" Mr. Cosby asked.

"Lauri's foster sister," Fat Albert explained. "Doris Robertson."

When Bill Cosby heard this name, he nearly fell off the porch. Could this really be happening, he wondered. Then, as he started making sense of things, a smile came over his face. "This is wonderful. I don't think I could've come up with something this good myself," he said.

"What do you mean?" asked Fat Albert.

"Okay," Mr. Cosby began, "but since I believed your story, you're going to have to believe mine."

Fat Albert nodded.

"You see, I based your character on this big kid named Albert, one of the kids I grew up with." Fat Albert was hanging on his every word. "The real Albert eventually got married, and had children and grandchildren," Mr. Cosby told him. Then, for what he was about to say, he made sure he spoke very slowly. "And my friend, Albert Robertson, particularly loved his only granddaughter, Doris. He used to help her with all her problems."

Fat Albert was amazed. "You mean there are two Doris Robertsons?"

Mr. Cosby corrected him. "Not two, Fat Albert," he explained carefully. "You see, in real life, my friend Albert's Doris Robertson and your Doris Robertson are the same person."

Albert thought on this for a moment. "But that would mean that Doris . . ." The possibility of the situation stopped him from finishing the sentence.

"That's right," Mr. Cosby said. "Doris Robertson is your granddaughter. And you came into this world to help her, because the real Albert is no longer with us," he explained. "But you have to go back into the television; because if you don't, you'll disappear completely. And then you'll never again be able to help all the people who love to watch you on television."

Fat Albert looked at Mr. Cosby and knew he was right. Then Fat Albert sighed, and tried to figure out how to do what he knew he had to.

# CHAPTER TEN
## *Why Me?* .

**L**auri was writing in her diary and had her brown teddy bear right next to her when she heard Albert's voice.

"Lauri!" he said in a loud whisper.

Startled, she turned toward her window, which was half open, and saw Fat Albert staring in. He had climbed up some lattice and was barely able to hang on.

"Albert, what are you doing here?" she asked.

"I need to talk to you," he told her. "It's very important."

"Okay. I'll meet you downstairs," she said. Then, without thinking, she started to close the window. Albert removed one hand, then the other, and before he knew what was happening, he was falling from the second story of Lauri's house. He landed with a thud on the walkway; it was times like these that he was glad to be a cartoon character. If he were human, he would have hurt himself for sure.

As Albert picked himself up, Lauri came dashing out the front door. "Are you okay?" she asked.

"Sure," he said. "For me, falling is easy. It's the getting up part that's hard."

Lauri laughed. "So what's this all about?"

On the walk over to her house, all Albert had thought about was the best way to tell her, but he still hadn't come up with anything. "Okay," he started. "You know what you said about me being your BFF?"

"And you are. My Best Friend Forever." Then Lauri smiled and took his hand.

Albert sighed when he felt his hand in hers. She certainly wasn't making this any easier. "See, the thing is," he continued, "I can't be your BFF. But I can be your BFUT."

Lauri had never heard that one before. "What does that mean?"

"Best Friend Until Tomorrow," he answered. "See, I have to leave tomorrow at two thirty."

"Leave? For where?" Lauri wanted to know.

When he saw her hurt expression, he decided he'd better get to the truth quickly. "Lauri, I know this will be hard for you to understand, but I don't just look like Fat Albert, I *am* Fat Albert."

"Why are you telling me this? I know who you are," she said.

"You don't understand. I'm really the guy in the cartoon," he said.

"What cartoon?" she asked innocently.

"*The Fat Albert Show*. Hey, hey, hey!"

"What are you talking about? Are you sure that roller coaster ride didn't scramble your brains?" she said.

"I'm not a real person," Fat Albert said. "I'm a cartoon character, and I live in a cartoon world. I thought maybe I could live in your world, but I can't; it's just not who I am. And if I don't go back into the TV tomorrow, I'm gonna disappear and never be seen again."

Lauri stared at Albert, her eyes filling with an angry hurt. "I've heard a lot of lame excuses for bailing out on a relationship, but that one takes the cake. You think I'm stupid?"

"Of course not, Lauri. I think you're wonderful. I care about you." And he realized that this would certainly be the most difficult thing he would ever have to do.

"Funny. Every time someone says they care about me, they wind up leaving me," she said angrily. Then she turned and ran toward the front door, on the verge of tears.

"But Danielle, you can't let fear . . ." Albert blurted.

Lauri stopped and turned to him. "Danielle? Who's that, your new girlfriend?" she asked.

"No. She's a girl in the cartoon," he explained. "Lauri, you can't let fear of getting hurt keep you from caring about someone."

"What do you know?" she asked.

"You're right. Since I never felt anything before, I never knew what it was like to have a person to think about," he admitted. "Or what it's like to have a person you think about also thinking about you. And I think it's fantastic to think that we'll both be thinking about each other."

Lauri stared at him for a second or two. "You know what I think?" she asked him. "I think that you need help!"

And with that, Lauri ran toward her house. But before she got there, Doris, who had come home earlier, opened the door from inside.

"Lauri, wait!" pleaded Fat Albert.

But Lauri didn't want to hear any more from him and

ran into the house. Doris looked at Fat Albert.

"You told her, didn't you?" she said, and Fat Albert nodded. "And you really expected her to believe you?" she asked.

"I hoped she would," he said. "I know I have to go, but if I could stay, you know what would be the best part? To have the opportunity to be the best that I was capable of being."

When Doris heard this, she stared at him for such a long time that Fat Albert became a bit uncomfortable.

"What?" he asked, bringing her back to her senses.

"I don't know," she said. "It's strange, but I just got the feeling that I know you. I mean, that I've known you . . . for a long, long time."

Fat Albert knew that now it was time to face this one. "You *have* known me for a long time," he began. Then he took Doris by the hand and they sat on a swing on the front porch. This one was going to take awhile.

Later, when Doris and Lauri were getting into bed, Lauri took the brown teddy bear from her bed and tossed it into the wastebasket.

"Don't do that, Lauri," said Doris. "Albert was telling you the truth."

"C'mon, Doris, don't tell me you believe that 'cartoon character' stuff," she said, shaking her head. "No one can come out of a television set."

"They did!" Doris insisted.

"Now they've got you believing it. You know what I think?" she warned. "I think they're some sort of a cult."

Doris sighed. "Trust me, Lauri. Some day you'll understand."

"Good night, Doris," Lauri replied, and turned off her light.

Doris looked at her, then went over to the wastebasket and retrieved the brown teddy bear and set it on the foot of Lauri's bed.

"Fat Albert never meant to hurt you," Doris said. Then she got into her bed and turned off the light. Although she knew she wouldn't do very well at tomorrow's track meet, she wanted to get some sleep, hard as that might be.

# CHAPTER ELEVEN

## *Day Three*

The next afternoon, the track meet was in full swing. On the infield, the pole-vaulters, the high jumpers, the long jumpers, and the shot-putters were doing their thing. And this wasn't just any track meet; today Ardsley High was facing its main rival, the team from Mt. Airy High School. On the track, the starting blocks were set up for the girls' four-hundred-meter run and Lauri, Doris, and four other runners from both schools were stepping into the blocks.

In the bleachers, Fat Albert, Bill, Rudy, and Mushmouth watched as the starter raised his pistol and fired a shot into the air. Filma, the star of the Mt. Airy girls' squad, blasted out of the blocks ahead of everyone. Lauri was second, a Mt. Airy girl was third, and Doris was fourth. But at the first turn, Doris overtook the Mt. Airy girl and moved into third place behind Filma and Lauri.

"Go Lauri!" "Nice move, Doris!" yelled the guys from the bleachers. It looked like it was going to be a very close race, because by the second turn, Lauri had gained on

Filma, and Doris was a strong third and moving up. But on the final turn, something happened. Although Lauri was only a stride behind Filma, Doris apparently lost her determination and began falling back; by the time they crossed the finish line, Filma was first, Lauri was second, and Doris was dead last.

Fat Albert and the guys leaped out of the bleachers and ran to Doris, who was not even breathing hard. "What happened?" asked Fat Albert. "You could have won that race."

Doris was shocked to see him. "Albert, what are you doing here?" Then she looked at the rest of them. "Look at yourselves. All of you are almost faded completely away."

But Fat Albert wasn't there to talk about himself. "You didn't even try. You gave up."

"Sixth is fine," she said, throwing on her sweats. "Now let's go. Your show has already started!"

And as they left the track stadium, Reggie and Arthur saw them go and decided to follow.

When they arrived back at the house, Doris hurried the guys into the family room and turned on the television.

Their show had started and the rest of their friends were calling to them from the cartoon junkyard.

"Hurry up, Fat Albert!" yelled Bucky. "Those other guys are coming back for a buck-buck match, and we don't stand a chance without you!"

Mushmouth moved to the screen. "Don't worry, Bucky, I'll be right there. And if those guys do come back before we all get there, I'll baffle them with some highfalutin language!" Then Mushmouth waved good-bye to Doris and plunged into the TV screen.

Mushmouth landed with a thud in the cartoon junkyard. As he picked himself up and dusted himself off, he noticed that all his color had returned. He turned to the screen. "Loobee! Iboo fiebee!"

"He said he's fine," explained Old Weird Harold as he looked into the screen. "Now come on, you guys. You're running out of time!"

In the family room, Rudy was the next to go. But before he stepped into the television, he turned to Doris. "Can I have a picture of us to take with me?"

"Sure," said Doris as she took the strip of black-and-white photos they took at the fair. But when she tried to hand them to Rudy, Fat Albert intercepted them.

"Sorry, Rudy, these pictures can't go into our world," he said. "They don't belong there."

Rudy understood. "That's okay," he told Doris. Then he tapped his head. "I have your picture right here. And right here, too." And then he tapped his heart, blew her a kiss, and glided into the television. And when he landed in the junkyard, he picked up an old chrome hubcap and used it for a mirror, and adjusted his hat just so.

Bill and Fat Albert were the last ones left in the human world. "Okay, you're next," said Fat Albert. "I just need a moment with Doris."

Bill considered this for a minute then nodded his acceptance. "Okay." Then he turned to Doris. "Thanks for everything."

"My pleasure," she said. "Take good care of yourself," and then, as she pointed at Fat Albert, ". . . and take care of him, too!"

Then Bill dove into the television set and landed near the convertible where Russell was standing. "Hey, Russell, I bet you're glad your big brother is back."

"You bet," said Russell. "Now I'm really gonna tell Mom on you!"

As Fat Albert and Doris laughed at this, they had no way of knowing that they were being watched by Reggie and Arthur, who were peering through the window.

Fat Albert looked at the television. "Well, I guess I'm going back to the way I was," he sighed.

"Nothing wrong with that," said Doris, smiling. Then she held her arms open wide and gave Fat Albert a big hug. "I love you, Grandpa."

"Hey, hey, hey!" he said. "You just get back to that track. You still have a relay to run!"

"It's no big deal. The team would do better without me," she said.

"Doris, that's not true. Now, go on," he said.

But Doris didn't move, and tears began to form as she took one final look at him. Somehow, Fat Albert knew what she was feeling.

"It's okay. I'll see you through the TV," he said with a big smile, trying to mask the sadness he was also feeling.

Doris wiped away her tears, and managed a weak smile

as she started for the door. "See ya," she said. And she waved to him as she walked out the door.

Albert sat on the sofa and buried his head in his hands. On the television screen, Bill peered out at him.

"C'mon, Fat Albert. Move it!" he yelled.

Fat Albert looked to the television, thinking. Then, like a lightning bolt, he figured it out. "Not yet," he said with newfound energy. "I came out to solve Doris's problem, but all I've done so far is hurt Lauri," he said as he opened the door to leave. He moved slowly, because the fading was sapping his strength.

From the cartoon junkyard, Bill urged him to reconsider. "But you won't be back in time," he said. "And you can't last another day."

"That's a chance I'll have to take. I just realized what Doris's problem really is. She sees herself as a loser. And losers can't win. Or let themselves have friends," he said. "Starting today," he continued, "that's going to change."

By now, all the guys were watching him through the screen. "Don't go," yelled Bucky.

"Yeah, man, you're gonna fade away," screamed Old Weird Harold.

"Webee neeboo youbee!" called Mushmouth.

But Fat Albert didn't want to hear what they had to say, so he shut off the TV and ran out.

At the track meet, the crowd was anxiously awaiting the final event: the girls' relay. And not only was it the final event, but it would also be the most important; the score was tied, and the team that won this race would also win the entire meet.

Doris's coach huddled the Ardsley High relay team together. "Okay, girls, this is it," he said. The four girls looked at one another, fully aware of what they had to do.

He put the baton in the hand of Yori, a very fast runner who always ran the first leg of the relay. Then he turned to Elisa, who normally ran the third leg. "Elisa," he said. "I've got a feeling about something. I want you to run the second leg today." Elisa nodded. "Lauri, you're up third. And Doris, I want you to bring it home for us." He walked away, leaving Doris flabbergasted.

"Me?" she gulped. "You're always the anchor," she said to Lauri. "How could Coach make me anchor?"

"Sorry, Doris, no more safety net for you. You're not a loser so stop behaving like one."

When the public address announcer called both teams to the starting line, Doris realized that she was about to run the most important race of her life, and she wasn't feeling very good about it.

The starter's pistol went off and Yori got off to a late start. At the first baton pass, she was several strides behind the Mt. Airy girl. Elisa, running second, tried to catch up, but couldn't. When she passed the baton, Lauri grabbed it and took off, still ten yards behind the Mt. Airy runner. But Lauri was determined, and ran with a rhythm that gradually narrowed the gap. As Doris prepared to receive the baton from Lauri, she looked over at the final Mt. Airy runner, the imposing Filma. Doris smiled at Filma weakly, but Filma just gave her a cold stare in return. By the final handoff, Lauri had caught up with the Mt. Airy runner and Doris and Filma received their batons at exactly the same instant.

But Filma soon began to pull away from Doris, and this only confirmed Doris' belief that Coach Gillespie made a huge mistake in naming her anchor. He should have gone with Lauri; Lauri's a winner. And as Filma extended her lead, Doris was resigned to losing once again.

But then, over the cheers of the Mt. Airy fans, she heard a voice. It was Fat Albert yelling, "Run, Doris!" Doris, who thought her mind was playing tricks on her, tried to block it out. But then she heard his voice again, and it much was closer this time. "You can win, Doris." She turned to see Fat Albert running right alongside her. But he wasn't running smoothly like before; he was struggling with every stride.

"What are you doing here?" she asked.

"I want to make sure you try," he panted. "Don't give up. You can do it, Doris. I know you can!"

But as Fat Albert became too tired to continue, Doris seemed to gain strength from his encouragement. As she focused on the back of Filma's jersey, Doris began striding with a strength and purpose that she didn't know she possessed. And gradually, she started gaining on Filma; she just hoped that Filma's lead wasn't too great to overcome. Doris poured every amount of concentration and energy into her effort and, as the finish line quickly approached, she was just one step behind! "Go for it, Doris. You can do this!" she told herself. And for the first time in her life, she actually believed it.

When the two girls were about to hit the tape, Doris somehow found the strength to lunge forward and cross the line only inches in front of Filma. Doris had really won! The crowd was cheering wildly, and the entire Ardsley team ran onto the track and lifted Doris to their shoulders. And although this was easily the happiest moment Doris had ever experienced, all she cared about was finding Fat Albert and getting him back into the television before the show ended. Doris got down from her teammates' shoulders, grabbed Lauri, and then the two of them ran toward the bleachers. When they approached, they saw that Fat Albert was breathing heavily and that his fading had entered a critical phase. Doris had to get him back to the television in time, or . . . Then she stopped herself; she didn't want to think about the "or."

"We've only got ten minutes," Doris said as she grabbed one of Albert's arms.

"Ten minutes for what?" asked Lauri.

"To get him back into the television before his show ends," she said.

"Oh, not that again," moaned Lauri.

"Look, just trust me on this," Doris said. "Now come on, I need your help."

Lauri took Fat Albert's other arm and together the two girls pulled him gently to his feet. But just as they started to walk him out of there, Reggie and Arthur suddenly appeared and blocked their path.

"So we meet again," Reggie said, taunting Fat Albert. "You're not looking so good, my man. What's wrong? Don't have the Cosby Kids here to help you?"

"Leave him alone," Doris said. "He's not feeling well."

"Aw, isn't that a shame." Reggie smiled; he was finally going to get revenge. Reggie turned to face the crowd still celebrating in the bleachers. "Hey, everybody!" he shouted. "Guess what? This fading fat fool isn't like the rest of us! He's Fat Albert, the guy from the cartoons!"

When the crowd heard this they began laughing at Reggie's foolishness, which only made him yell louder. "I mean it! He's not real," Reggie insisted. "He came out of a television set!" But the crowd ignored Reggie and his silliness.

"Move, Reggie, we've got to go," said Doris as she and Lauri tried to get Fat Albert out of there.

"Oh, no. Fat man is not going anywhere," he said, putting his hand to Albert's chest. Then he looked into Fat Albert's eyes, which were barely open. "It's you and me, large one. Man to man."

And then, before Reggie could do anything about it, Fat Albert opened his eyes fully and used his last bit of energy to pick Reggie up and lift him above his shoulders. "You heard the lady," Fat Albert said. "So hey, hey, hey, get out of our way!" And as he set Reggie down, Reggie was so stunned that he and Arthur could only watch as the girls helped Fat Albert out of the bleachers and away from there.

As they reached the sidewalk in front of the school, the girls struggled to get Fat Albert to walk faster, but he just didn't have the strength. Then Lauri saw a boy she knew riding his skateboard, and dashed over to him.

"Hey, Derrick, can I borrow your board for a few minutes?"

"No problem," he said, and handed her his skateboard.

Then she and Doris propped up Fat Albert on the skateboard and began rolling him home as fast as they could go. And although Lauri still didn't believe a word of Albert's story about being a cartoon character, it was clear that he needed help. And that was good enough for her.

And though they were moving at a good speed, Doris knew that time was running out—the show would be over in three minutes! But it was downhill the rest of the way to her house, so maybe they still had a chance, even though the traffic signal just ahead of them suddenly turned red. While they waited for the light to change, Doris momentarily released Albert's arm to wipe the perspiration from her forehead, not realizing that Lauri had done the same thing.

With nothing holding him back, Albert began rolling downhill; and before the girls realized their mistake, he was in the middle of the street, directly in the path of an oncoming truck! The girls closed their eyes, and when they opened them they expected to see that Fat Albert had become Flat Albert! But miraculously, the truck had somehow missed him, and Fat Albert was still on the skateboard, careening down the steep decline that led to Doris's house.

As Doris and Lauri gave chase, they saw a man pushing a flower cart, unaware that Albert was approaching from behind. Before the girls could shout a warning, Albert crashed into the man and his cart, sending flowers flying everywhere. But Albert was able to maintain his balance and stay on the board. He continued speeding downhill, even though he now had a rose in his mouth and three daisies in his hair! As he approached Doris's house, Fat Albert was so totally out of control that he went over a curb, off a fire hydrant, and then smashed into Doris's front door.

When the girls reached him, they found him woozy but smiling.

"Are you okay?" Doris asked.

Albert, who was growing weaker by the second, found the energy to say, "Hey, hey, hey. Flying is easy; it's the landing that's hard." And then, with a sheepish grin, he gave Lauri the rose and Doris the three daisies.

Then the girls helped Fat Albert to his feet and led him inside. The clock on the wall indicated that they still had two minutes left when Doris grabbed the remote and switched on the television. The guys were gathered at the screen and peered out at them. "It's about time, man!" Bill said to Fat Albert. And then Bill climbed halfway into the room to help his friend back into the television. Lauri saw this and screamed; then she staggered backwards and fell over the couch, disappearing behind it.

"Come on, let's go!" Bill said as he pulled Albert toward the TV. "The show's just about over."

"I'm coming," Albert promised, just as Lauri peeked over the back of the couch in time to see Fat Albert push Bill back into the television.

Although Lauri had a hard time believing what she was witnessing, she came out from behind the couch. "You were telling the truth," she said to Fat Albert.

"I knew you'd believe me some day," he said. "I never meant to hurt you, Lauri. I love you." He wanted to touch her one last time, but Doris stopped him and brought him back to the television.

"You have to go, Albert. Now," she said.

Albert knew she was right and started climbing into the television.

"Albert, wait. I don't understand any of this," Lauri told him. "But will you ever come back?"

"If there's any way I can, you can count on it," he said. "But either way, we'll always have the memories."

"And I'll always have my Big Al," Lauri told him, fighting back tears. "I just found out that caring about someone is wonderful. And I never want to not feel again." Then Lauri walked over to Albert and gave him a soft, tender kiss on the lips.

Fat Albert let that kiss sink in, then reached into his back pocket, removed his 76ers cap, and gave it to Lauri. "I have to go now. But I'll send you a special signal so you'll know I'm always thinking about you," he said. Then he winked with his left eye as he said, "Hey." Then he winked with his right eye, saying "hey" again. And then, with a final wink of his left eye, he ended with the third "hey."

And while the girls held each other for comfort, Fat Albert gathered every bit of strength he had left, and climbed into the television.

And just like that, he was gone.

The girls watched Albert land in the cartoon junkyard, and allowed themselves relieved smiles when all his bright color and energy immediately came back.

"Now," Fat Albert said to Russell and the others, "I understand that someone wants to play buck-buck!" When the tough teenagers saw Fat Albert lumbering toward them, they ran away as fast as they could, never to be seen again.

As Fat Albert and the guys celebrated, they noticed Danielle passing by.

"Danielle, wait!" Fat Albert yelled as they all ran to her.

"What do you want?" she asked.

"You can't quit school and run away," he said.

"What's it to you?" she demanded, exactly like before.

"I care about you," he told her.

"Well, don't. Every time someone says they care about me, they wind up leaving me," she said coldly.

"But Danielle, you can't let fear . . ." he said, stopping just as before. But this time, he decided to continue. "You can't let fear keep you from caring about someone, because caring about someone is beautiful."

"Hey, wait a minute," Danielle protested, "that's not in the script."

"That didn't come from the writers; that came from me," he explained. "You see, everyone needs a person to think about and have that person think about them. And it's just fantastic to know that you're thinking about each other. Believe me, I know."

Danielle's eyes began to mist over. "That's beautiful," she told him.

"Thank you," he said. Then, just as the show was ending, he turned and looked directly into the television. "Hey, hey, hey!" he said, quickly blinking his left eye, then his right, and finally his left again.

And in the family room . . . Lauri cried. But her tears were more out of happiness than sadness, because she knew that she would never again refuse to let herself get close to someone. Albert was right; it really was good to know that someone was out there thinking about you.

And Doris made a vow to herself that from now on, she would only think of herself as a winner. And she believed it, too, because after that relay race anything was possible . . . even making new friends.

Then the two foster sisters—and best friends—hugged each other tight, knowing that everything that had happened would have to remain their own little secret, because no one would ever, ever believe their story.

As they left the room, Doris switched off the television set and Lauri put on Albert's 76ers cap. Then they turned out the lights, knowing that a group of ragtag cartoon characters had come into their world and changed their lives forever.

# *EPILOGUE*

That evening, the family was having dinner together because Doris's father had returned from his business trip. "So, Doris," Mr. Robertson said, "I heard you were the star of the track meet today."

"Not really, Daddy," Doris said meekly. "It wasn't a big deal."

When Lauri heard that, she cleared her throat loudly and gave Doris a scolding look. Had she already forgotten the lesson she learned from Fat Albert?

Doris smiled, "Actually, Dad, it was a big deal. Coach made me the anchor in the four-by-four relay, and I was running against a girl from Mt. Airy named Filma, who is Little Miss Track Star over there. And even though she started with a lead, I beat her. Not by much, but I beat her!" she said, still trying to be modest.

"And because of Doris," Lauri continued, "we won the meet!"

"That's wonderful, sweetheart," her father said. "I'm sorry I missed that."

"Don't worry about it, Dad," Doris replied. "I have a

feeling I'm gonna do it again next week."

And she and Lauri slapped high fives across the table as Mr. and Mrs. Robertson smiled, taking notice of this change in their daughter.

"So what else happened around here while I was gone?" he asked. "Anything interesting?"

"Interesting?" Doris asked as she and Lauri exchanged mischievous glances. "I can't think of anything," she said. "Can you, Lauri?"

"Nope," Lauri answered quickly. "Not a thing. Nothing interesting ever happens around here."

And as the family resumed their dinner, Lauri looked at Doris and blinked her left eye, then her right, then her left again.